D0866749

BEHIND the EYES

ALSO BY

FRANCISCO X. STORK

The Way of the Jaguar

DUTTON BOOKS

BEHIND

FRANCISCO X. STORK

the EYES

D U T T O N   B O O K S / A division of Penguin Young Readers Group

PUBLISHED BY THE PENGUIN GROUP

Penguin Group (USA) Inc., 375 Hudson Street, New York, New York 10014, U.S.A. / Penguin Group (Canada), 90 Eglinton Avenue East, Suite 700, Toronto, Ontario, Canada M4P 2Y3 (a division of Pearson Penguin Canada Inc.) / Penguin Books Ltd, 80 Strand, London WC2R 0RL, England / Penguin Ireland, 25 St Stephen's Green, Dublin 2, Ireland (a division of Penguin Books Ltd) / Penguin Group (Australia), 250 Camberwell Road, Camberwell, Victoria 3124, Australia (a division of Pearson Australia Group Pty Ltd) / Penguin Books India Pvt Ltd, 11 Community Centre, Panchsheel Park, New Delhi - 110 017, India / Penguin Group (NZ), Cnr Airborne and Rosedale Roads, Albany, Auckland 1310, New Zealand (a division of Pearson New Zealand Ltd) / Penguin Books (South Africa) (Pty) Ltd, 24 Sturdee Avenue, Rosebank, Johannesburg 2196, South Africa / Penguin Books Ltd, Registered Offices: 80 Strand, London WC2R 0RL, England

This book is a work of fiction. Names, characters, places, and incidents are either the product of the author's imagination or are used fictitiously, and any resemblance to actual persons, living or dead, business establishments, events, or locales is entirely coincidental.

The publisher does not have any control over and does not assume any responsibility for author or third-party websites or their content.

Poem on pages vi–vii, "Light Breaks Where No Sun Shines," by Dylan Thomas, from THE POEMS OF DYLAN THOMAS, copyright © 1939 by New Directions Publishing Corp. Reprinted by permission of New Directions Publishing Corp.

CIP Data is available.

Published in the United States by Dutton Books, a member of Penguin Group (USA) Inc., 345 Hudson Street, New York, New York 10014 / www.penguin.com/youngreaders

Printed in USA / Designed by Heather Wood

ISBN 0-525-47735-7   10 9 8 7 6 5 4 3 2 1   First Edition

*For
Nicholas
& Anna*

Acknowledgments: The writing of a novel, I have come to find out, is both a solitary and a communal labor. Without guidance, it is easy to end up with a child that is either misdirected or undeveloped. So I am grateful for those who generously helped to write *Behind the Eyes* "with me": Faye Bender, my agent, friend, the other half of the creative endeavor; Stephanie Owens Lurie, my editor, who wrung out of me the hidden beauty in Hector's story; Sergeant Kelly, formerly of the LAPD, for his advice in the portrayal of gang life; my author-friend Patricia Santana for her incisive and sensitive reading of the initial manuscript; and Keren Schlomy for her meticulous proofreading. But most of all I am grateful to Jill Syverson-Stork, my wife, for sharing with me her sound literary instincts and giving me her hope.

Light breaks where no sun shines;

Where no sea runs, the waters of the heart

Push in their tides;

And, broken ghosts with glow-worms in their heads,

The things of light

File through the flesh where no flesh decks the bones.

A candle in the thighs

Warms youth and seed and burns the seeds of age;

Where no seed stirs,

The fruit of man unwrinkles in the stars,

Bright as a fig;

Where no wax is, the candle shows its hairs.

Dawn breaks behind the eyes;

From poles of skull and toe the windy blood

Slides like a sea;

Nor fenced, nor staked, the gushers of the sky

Spout to the rod

Divining in a smile the oil of tears.

Night in the sockets rounds,

Like some pitch moon, the limit of the globes;

Day lights the bone;

Where no cold is, the skinning gales unpin

The winter's robes;

The film of spring is hanging from the lids.

Light breaks on secret lots,

On tips of thought where thoughts smell in the rain;

When logics die,

The secret of the soil grows through the eye,

And blood jumps in the sun;

Above the waste allotments the dawn halts.

—DYLAN THOMAS

BEHIND
the
EYES

BOOK one

1

Hector missed his brother's wake. He missed the funeral. Dr. Hernández, the intern who treated him in the emergency room, had told him it would be at least a week before he could leave. The ear, the ribs, the spleen, all had to be evaluated. All needed stillness in order to begin to heal.

Part of Hector felt relieved. It was comfortable and safe in the hospital, even though he shared a room with two other patients. One of them, a skinny and unshaven older man, kept staring at him as if trying to recognize him. Hector could close his eyes and try to forget all that had happened. The throbbing in his head, the pinching in his chest, the numbness of his back, were almost welcome distractions. Images of his sister and mother alone at the funeral home, or standing beside an open grave, he tried to brush away.

During their first visit, when their mother was in the bathroom, Hector asked his sister, Aurora, not to bring Mamá again. It was too hard for her to see him in this state. It wasn't worth it. He'd be out in a few days. Keep her home. But Aurora's knowing smile told Hector that she saw right through him. It was hard for *Hector* to see Mamá. She brought him the knowledge that he had gone and made things worse.

Now Mrs. Garza, the social worker, was here to remind him yet again. She sat down in the chair beside his bed, then got up to draw the curtain that separated Hector from the old man who had fixed his eyes unwaveringly on them. Mrs. Garza's expression told Hector that she was bringing bad news but was trying to look on the bright side. She edged her chair closer to the bed. She cleared her throat. She was about to deliver important information. His heart beat faster. He felt a sticky dampness on his palms.

"Hector." He could tell she was wondering whether she should come straight to the point. "I've been talking to the police, and their informants. We've heard that the Discípulos have a marker on your life." She had decided to come straight to the point. She paused to see if he understood.

Hector felt himself go pale, as if someone had pulled plugs in the soles of his feet and the blood had drained out. He nodded slightly.

She went on. "It's complicated—part of gang politics that doesn't make sense to outsiders. The Discípulos have been trying to ally themselves with a local branch of the Mejicanos, an L.A. gang. Chava has been working on this alliance for a while now. Apparently he needs their help against the Indians, who have allied themselves with a local chapter of the Cribs. Anyway, Chava has decided that there is disrespect against him that needs to be addressed. Chava says it's not business anymore, it's personal. He thinks his leadership is in question as long as you're around. But you are too small a fish for him to come after directly. So he has put a marker on you. Oh, shit. These kids . . ." Her voice began to squeak, as if something were tightening around her throat.

Hector, too, found it hard to breathe. He had spent his whole life trying to avoid being a mark of any sort, and now here he was, being singled out in the worst possible way.

"Hector, listen to me. I want you to know the whole truth." He heard her words in the distance, as if she were speaking to him through the window of a departing train. "It's not just what you did. The way Filiberto died put Chava in a bad light. It made it seem as if Chava was a coward. He's lost face."

Hector was reminded of what Filiberto had said to him that night at El Corralito. Something about letting Chava save face. How could things have turned out so wrong?

"Are you listening to me, Hector?" Mrs. Garza leaned closer.

"Yes," he answered listlessly. He was incredibly tired.

He felt her shake his arm before he realized she had been repeating his name. "Hector, Hector. We're going to get you out of this. We have a plan. You hear me?" She was practically yelling, perhaps to compensate for the bandage on his ear.

"It's not safe for you to stay in El Paso anymore. I found a place in San Antonio that I want you to consider. It's a school for kids who have gotten into trouble but show promise of rehabilitation. It's a good, good place, Hector. It's a model for other schools of this type."

With what seemed like a huge effort, Hector turned his head away.

"It costs money, but I'm confident we can get funding for your tuition. There wouldn't be any burden on your mother."

Hector closed his eyes. No husband for the past year; now no sons . . . She was more burdened than anyone he knew, and nothing would ever change that.

"I have already spoken to her, and Aurora," Mrs. Garza continued. "They'll miss you, of course, but they know it's the only way for you to be safe."

Hector turned back to look at Mrs. Garza. She acted as though it was all so simple. "What about their safety?" he croaked as he tried to untangle himself from the sheet twisted around his sore torso.

"The Discípulos won't put a marker on Aurora or Conchita. They don't operate that way. It's you they're after, and this school in San Antonio—Furman—will offer you protection. More than that, it will give you a future. You can get your high school diploma, and apply to college after that . . ."

College. Hector felt tears coming on as he remembered what Filiberto had told him about Papá and the college fund.

Mrs. Garza misread his face. "Hector, I know the prospect of leaving home is scary, but there's something you need to accept. *You* went after Chava. If you hadn't been stopped, you would have killed him."

Hector choked back the tears. They tasted like blood.

"You'll have to go through a formal hearing where you'll

plead guilty to assault. We're assuming——because it's a first offense—the judge will give you probation. Having some-place to go, like Furman, will help your case. Furman takes kids who have gotten into trouble with the law, but only if they have a future. It may not be a fancy boarding school where everyone wears a jacket and tie—those places wouldn't touch you—but it isn't jail, either."

"What does Aurora think?" Hector asked.

"She wants what's best for you, Hector. She told me about your dad and Fili, and about you, about how smart you are. You have gone through an awful lot, and right now the projects aren't the best place for you. You need a place where you can grow and develop safely. I talked to the head of Furman. He said that kids who are forced to go there usually don't make it. They only want kids who choose to come. *You* need to decide, not Aurora, or your mother, or me. If you don't want to go, we'll come up with another way of protecting you from the Discípulos. Hector, do you hear me?"

I'm not totally deaf, he felt like telling her. What he didn't hear was not because his ear was shot to hell. There was no point in listening. He had no choices, no future. He was as good as dead, sooner or later, whenever, wherever.

Mrs. Garza got up to leave, a look of exhaustion on her face. Standing next to his bed, she said, "The doctor says you can leave tomorrow, after they fit you for a hearing aid. If you decide to go to Furman, we should push through with the process right away. How about I come tomorrow to take you home? You can let me know then."

Hector closed his eyes again, but he felt her waiting there. She wanted some sort of acknowledgment, something to take with her. He didn't look at her as she walked away. He was too tired to lift his eyelids, which had never felt so heavy.

2

Hector sat on the hood of a car parked on the street. He had managed to leave the apartment without waking Aurora or his mother. Dawn was breaking through in slow motion, turning the black sky to a steely gray. Here and there a few lights flickered inside the apartments. On a normal day, Hector would be heading over to church to help Father Ochoa by now. In the past year he had not missed a single six o'clock Mass. Now he was going to miss every morning.

Hector had started going to church after his father died. He wasn't sure why, but one day he got up on his own to go to Mass with his mother. Conchita didn't seem all that surprised, although it had never happened before. "Ah, Hector, *vienes a misa? Qué bueno.*" That's all she said. Nor did she seem surprised when he kept doing it, morning after morning.

Before long he became an altar boy. He didn't understand what had possessed him. Maybe he secretly liked the admiration of his mother and her friends, the only people who knew he was doing it. They all thought he'd become a priest for sure. After Mass he had to sneak out the back way to avoid "the Crows," as he thought of Conchita's three companions. Otherwise they'd peck him to death with their questions about his sacred destiny.

Or maybe he was making some kind of deal with a make-believe God: *I'll get up early every day and help out if You look out for me.* Now he snorted at the thought.

In the distance he heard the mellow sound of the old church bell, which Father Ochoa always rang at 5:45. The few times Hector had arrived early, Father Ochoa let him ring the bell. Six slow pulls of the rope made twelve *bong*s as the bell's iron clapper hit each side. How ironic it seemed for the same person to be an altar boy and a would-be killer. And yet the two conflicting images were connected, like the double *bong* of the bell's clapper.

A brown-and-white car with red and blue cherry lights turned onto his street. It parked in front of him and an officer stepped out.

"Hector Robles?"

Hector's "yes" took a while to surface through the fog in his mind.

"I'm Jerry Mulligan," said the officer. Hector pretended not to see the officer's extended hand as he bent down to pick up his suitcase.

"You can put that in the backseat and sit up front."

Hector wondered if he had to. Was he now "in custody"? He still didn't really understand what it meant to be on probation. Usually "perps" had to sit in the back, and that's where he'd rather be. "Uh, could I stretch out in the back for a while? I need to get some sleep." Hector slid into the backseat without waiting for an answer.

"Suit yourself," said Jerry Mulligan. "But if I doze off and crash, it'll be your fault."

Add it to the list, Hector thought. They drove in silence past the old church. His mother would miss six o'clock Mass because of him. He'd turned off her alarm clock so he wouldn't have to face her or Aurora this morning. After he'd thought about it for close to an hour, he wrote a note that said, *I'll write soon.* It was all he could write. Words no longer came easily to him.

"I'm sorry about your brother," said Jerry Mulligan.

Hector stiffened. The last thing he wanted to do was talk, especially about this, especially with Jerry Mulligan.

"I was the one who came to tell your mother about his . . . the accident."

Hector moved closer to the window, out of the range of the officer's eyes in the rearview mirror. *Just shut the hell up,* he pleaded silently.

"It was the first time I ever had to tell anyone, you know, inform them that a relative had died."

Mulligan proceeded to explain in detail how he'd been elected to do the dirty deed, and Hector tuned him out, relieved that the officer wasn't interested in probing. He just liked to hear himself talk.

But he had painted an ugly picture in Hector's mind, of Aurora waking up to a knock on the door.

She stumbles out of bed, half-asleep. She thinks dreamily that it's Filiberto—he must have lost his keys again. The last time it happened, she opened the door and no one was there. Then she looked down and saw Filiberto on his knees, drunk. It didn't bother her. She was used to it.

The knocking persists. *Why is it,* she thinks, *that I am the only one who wakes up to knocking in the middle of the night? Why can't Hector ever get up?*

13

When she opens the door, she is surprised to see a man in a brown sheriff's uniform. "Hi," he says awkwardly. "Are your parents home?"

Now it dawns on her that she opened the door without checking to see who it was. The man looks friendly, but you can't trust anyone in the projects.

"My mother and brothers are here."

"Your brothers?"

She hesitates. She had seen Hector studying before she went to bed, but Filiberto may not have come home. Still, it was better to be safe and say that both of them are in. She answers, "Yes."

"I'm from the sheriff's department. May I speak to your mother?"

Aurora turns, dread building in her stomach, and walks down the hall, past Mamá's bedroom, and into her brothers' room. The two beds are empty, and she immediately knows something bad has happened. Just like that day at school, when they called her into the office to tell her that Papá had died.

Aurora wishes she didn't have to wake up Mamá. She wishes she could spare her the sadness that was coming. She wishes she could convince the kind-looking officer that she was old enough to bear the bad news alone. She is the one in the family who knew how to take care of problems, after all—problems like the Discípulos and all the trouble the Gloria girl had gotten them into. The men don't know how to deal with problems. They either hide from them, like Hector, or use too much force against them, like Filiberto, or allow themselves to be chewed up and swallowed by them, like Papá. The men don't know how to ask for help.

"Mamá, wake up." Aurora gently shakes her mother's shoulder.

Conchita opens her eyes and sits up. *"Ya es hora?"* she asks.

"There's a man outside. A policeman. He wants to talk to you."

"Qué?" Conchita swings her legs out of the bed, almost hitting Aurora. She grabs her tattered pink robe and sticks her feet into the purple, furry slippers Aurora gave her for Mother's Day. She is at the front door in a flash.

"My God, what is it? What happened?" asks Mamá.

"Evening, ma'am." The officer raises his hand to his temple as if saluting her. "Does Filiberto Robles live here?"

"Yes," Aurora responds. "But he is not home right now. I thought he was. Neither of my brothers are."

"Qué dice? Qué, qué?" Conchita turns to Aurora, asking for an interpretation. All of a sudden she can't understand a word of English. *"Qué pasa, Aurora? Qué ha pasado?"*

"What is this about? Do you know where Hector and Filiberto are?" Aurora asks the deputy.

"Okay. Filiberto has been in an accident. I don't know anything about a Hector. As far as I know, only one person was in the car. We think it was Filiberto Robles. Your mother needs to come over to the hospital with me. You can come, too."

"Qué, qué? Ay, Díos mio. Filiberto? Dónde está Hector?"

Hector winced. The worry his mother must have felt when she discovered his absence pained him still. But now she wouldn't have to worry anymore. Aurora could finally sleep through the night without hearing any knocking on the door.

It was the only reason he had decided to go to Furman.

3

Colonel Taylor's impeccably neat office, complete with American flag, added to Hector's impression that he was entering boot camp. On his arrival Hector had learned that Furman was situated on an old air-force base. The dorms were long, aluminum sheds where the airmen used to live. Classes were held in a cinderblock building that used to be the base's administrative headquarters. The gym was a converted airplane hangar.

Furman's headmaster, Hal Taylor, was a retired air-force colonel. On the dark paneled walls of his office Hector saw pictures of men dressed in jumpsuits, white aviator helmets dangling by their side, standing in front of fighter jets. Clearly the man had never let go of his past. As the Colonel delivered his speech from behind his desk, Hector wondered if it was the same one he had given to incoming cadets.

"Let me inform you of the ground rules," he began, staring intently at Hector.

Hector did his best to return his steady gaze, trying not to blink first, but in the end he had to look away. After the ten-hour drive, he was too exhausted to play this kind of game.

In a forceful, authoritative tone that Hector would expect from the head of a military school, Colonel Taylor told him about the mandatory buzz haircuts and the regulation gray shorts and gray T-shirts everyone wore day and night. Six days a week the schedule consisted of a 6:00 A.M. wake-up call followed by marching and calisthenics; one half hour for breakfast; classes; one half hour for lunch; more classes; work detail; organized outdoor recreation; one hour for dinner; study time; and lights-out at 10:00 P.M. On Sundays the students were "treated" to an inspirational talk delivered by a guest lecturer or the Colonel himself. Students also met with their counselors on Sundays, and occasionally—if everyone on a given team had fulfilled all of their responsibilities—they could go on field trips. The day of rest was capped off with a movie or two hours of television.

Radios or boom boxes were not allowed in the bunks, but CD players with headphones could be used during quiet time. Computers were used for research only; there was no e-mail access. Cell phones were not permitted. Students could not make outgoing phone calls, but they could receive one call per week. Letter writing was encouraged.

Hector had no problem with the isolation. It made him feel safer. He didn't expect to receive any phone calls, because no one back home (except the judge, Mrs. Garza, and Deputy Sheriff Jerry Mulligan) knew where he was. Neither Conchita nor Aurora had his phone number or address—they hadn't even been told the name of the school. Mrs. Garza had agreed to act as Hector's personal postmaster and make sure any written correspondence got to or from him.

What Hector worried about most was living 24/7 with bunkmates. More than anything he craved solitude. He felt no attachment to anyone anymore, and he wanted to keep it that way. But the Colonel had said something about teams. Hector wondered what that meant.

"Regardless of how you got here," Colonel Taylor was saying, "the fact is that it is a privilege to be here. Someone is paying a lot of money—about one hundred dollars a day—so you can be here. The one thing we cannot do is waste that money. If you don't accept the privilege of being here, then that privilege will be given to someone who will. It's a matter of simple economics. You are here because someone thinks there is a high probability that you will not only turn your life around, but you will make a positive contribution to your country."

Hector resisted the urge to roll his eyes—or salute. He wondered how much the Colonel knew about his background. No one expected anything of him. They just didn't want any more trouble.

"We can't justify spending this kind of money on a juvenile delinquent when there are good kids out there who aren't getting the kind of education that you'll be getting here."

Hector hadn't felt like a juvenile delinquent until the day he went to court. Kids and teenagers of various ages lined the halls of the courthouse. He saw eyes gleaming with spite, eyes clouded by drugs. Adult relatives huddled in corners, lost, waiting for someone who knew how the system worked to tell them where to go, what to do, what had happened. As soon as Hector entered the courtroom, it was obvious that everyone there saw him as a heartless criminal, unquestionably guilty of aggravated assault. The extenuating circumstances didn't matter. He was a menace to society, a burden on the system, someone to get rid of. His mother consented to send him away for a year. His sister, Aurora, had even said they would be better off without him.

Did she feel that way about Papá? And Filiberto? If anyone was a juvenile delinquent, it was him. Filiberto had been delinquent even as a child.

Filiberto is ten years old and Hector is six. Filiberto is pulling Hector in a red wagon, the same steel wagon Conchita uses to haul groceries from the Piggly Wiggly. Filiberto is taking him to the irrigation ditch that waters the cotton fields.

At the ditch they find a group of Anglo kids making and exploding firecrackers. They are older and bigger than Filiberto. They place the shell upright on a flat rock and then, in one motion, heave another rock toward it while running in the opposite direction. Most of the time the rock misses.

Filiberto laughs at the kids and calls them names—sissies, chickens without any guts. Two big kids come over with a rock, and Hector thinks they are going to throw it at Filiberto. Instead they toss it at Filiberto's feet and say something to him in English that Hector doesn't understand. Filiberto tosses their rock away and finds a different one—round and smooth, the size of his hand. He kneels beside the firecracker, straightens it. He lifts his stone high in the air; then he looks at the Anglo kids and laughs. They move back, covering their ears. Filiberto slams the shell with the stone, and the shell explodes with a bang that rattles the wagon where Hector's sitting. Hector's ears are ringing when he opens his eyes to see Filiberto laughing and offering his stone to the other kids.

They all step back. Filiberto insults them again. *"Maricones!"* he yells.

One of the kids—the biggest one—finally takes the stone. He has a crew cut and a white-and-red striped shirt that reminds Hector of a parade. His forehead is muddy with sweat and the dirt from the ditch. He places another firecracker upright on the flat rock, stretching as far away from the shell as he possibly can. His eyes are shut when he raises his hand and then lets the rock fall. He doesn't strike the shell with much force, and when it explodes, it doesn't bang as loud as the other one.

Hector opens his eyes when he hears the kid screaming. The five fingertips that gripped the stone are gushing blood, their tops blown open. The kid is jumping up and down, shouting, holding the bleeding hand up in the air, like a Fourth of July sparkler. Blood sprinkles his face and shirt. No one knows what to do. Everyone is moving around like angry ants. Some of the kids are yelling at the boy with the bleeding hand, others are yelling at Filiberto, calling him wetback, blaming him. Filiberto grabs another rock and waves it at them. He has that grin and that look of his. He challenges the kids to come closer so he can crack their skulls open.

The kids back away, all huddled in a group, a bleeding hand sticking out from the middle. They move in a swarm toward their houses and fenced-in yards and aboveground swimming pools.

Hector didn't understand Filiberto at the time, or even when he was older. But now he knew there was something useful about the hatred Filiberto had for those who belonged and passed judgment on those who did not. Hatred provided courage and strength and, like love, a kind of solace. When you hated, you did not feel lonely.

4

"**Hey, man, you interested** in some pussy?" were the first words X-Lax spoke to Hector.

X-Lax was Hector's roommate. Hector never learned his real name and suspected the nickname had something to do with the fact that X-Lax was always running off at the mouth, even when no one was listening.

He started talking the moment Hector plunked his ugly suitcase on the floor of Room 4-B, Dormitory C. X-Lax, lanky, jellyfish white, with a grin that looked as if it had been drawn with a pink crayon, was on the bottom bunk.

"It's fake pussy for now, but I'm working on getting me

the real kind soon enough. Come over here, bro, just step over here and let me show you my fine merchandise." X-Lax opened the bottom drawer of his desk and took out a stash of magazines. "Look here. I got all kinds—*Playboy, Penthouse, Hustler,* you name it. You can borrow yourself any one of these for only twenty-five cents an evening. 'Course I'd have to charge you extra if you go and stain them."

"No, thanks."

"Well, okay. You'll change your mind. Where you from?"

"Around."

"You here for long?"

"Yeah, for long."

"Man, you must be badass bad. What you do?"

"I beat the crap out of someone," Hector said menacingly.

"Oooh. Down, boy, down. I'm a lover, not a fighter. What's your name, anyway?"

"Hector."

"What the heck, Hecktor. Don't worry about it, Mr. Heck. This place ain't so bad. Like Chicken Wings just finished telling you, it's a privy-lege to be here. One year'll go by 'fore you know it. You feel free to rent some of my ladies anytime you want."

Hector sat on one of the two chairs in the room, the one

at the unoccupied desk. He pulled his unused hearing aid out of his pocket and put it on the desk, wishing he really were deaf right now.

"What'd you bring?" X-Lax asked, pointing at the suitcase. "You got any goodies of your own? Come on, open that sucker up. Share and share alike, that's the Furman roomie code."

Hector didn't move.

"Hey, man, you hungry? You know, if we go down to the cafeteria, I think I can get you some chow. We all eat at five, but there's leftovers I can get you. Let's go."

"I'm not hungry," said Hector.

"Suit yourself. I wasn't in any hurry to start eating slop either when I first got here." X-Lax opened another drawer in his desk and took out a stash of Baby Ruths. "Don't tell anyone I have these. I'm telling you, people here think chocolate is worse than drugs. They can handle a doped-up kid, but a kid all hyped up on sugar? Man, that's a real danger, know what I'm saying?"

Surely the kid would stop talking sooner or later if Hector just ignored him. He stared at his old suitcase, the same one his mother had brought from Mexico when she first came to the States. Hector was sure it had not been used in the twenty years since it first crossed the Rio Grande.

X-Lax was still talking. "The hardest part about this

place is the nights. It's lights-out at ten, but the lights in here"—he pointed to his head—"don't necessarily go out at ten, know what I'm saying?" X-Lax reached under his bunk and pulled out a boom box the size of a small child. Hector wondered how he had managed to bring and keep so much forbidden paraphernalia. So much for tight security at Furman. "We're supposed to turn these off at ten, but no one cares if you use earphones."

X-Lax dangled his earphones in front of Hector, a sly smile across his face. Then he got off the bunk and peered at the hearing aid. "Hey, man, you're handy-dandy-capped," he exclaimed, as if it were cause for celebration. "I'm handy-dandy-capped, too! Give me five." Hector only looked at X-Lax's hand.

X-Lax sat down on his bunk again and leaned toward Hector. "I only got one ball. No shit, man! I'd show it to you, but I don't know you that well yet and I'm unsure of your ooorientation, sexual-wise, if you follow my meaning. What happened was this: When I was nothing but a little kid, my so-called biological father kicked me so hard that one of my nuts traveled up somewhere deep, and ever since then it has refused to come down. Can't say I blame it. Hey, I wonder if that's why Colonel Chicken Wings put us together, us both being handy-dandy-capped and all. Chicken Wings and his nuggets are always thinking, thinking. They anal-ize every little detail of our miserable lives. They plot and scheme about ways to make us outstanding citizens. I shit you not! They have meetings every week—the RAs and the RMs and the rest of the Nortons—and they talk about how so-and-so is coming along and who's not getting along with who and how Johnny Q's down in the dumps, and then they try maneuvering things. 'Let's put Johnny Q in this class and have him do a project with Pepe the Fart to get him out of his funk.' I shit you not!"

Hector was beginning to feel dizzy. "Is there a bathroom around here?" he asked.

X-Lax pointed at the sink in the room. "There's that. The shit holes—otherwise known as the number two receptacles—are down the hall to the right."

By a stroke of luck, X-Lax was not in the room when Hector returned from the bathroom. He took the opportunity to unpack without prying eyes. Most of the drawers in the dresser were already full of magazines, CDs, batteries, Polaroids (some normal, some lewd), letters that smelled like dead flowers, and unopened bags of Baby Ruths. But he found two empty drawers and shoved in the clothes his mother had packed for him. The day before he left the hospital she and Aurora had gone shopping at Kmart. There were six pairs of tube socks; six size 36 briefs (one size too large); six gray crewneck T-shirts; two pairs of athletic shorts; blue jeans; a white short-sleeved shirt; a sweatshirt; and a pair of blue pajamas he knew he would never wear. Underneath the clothes he found a small portable radio with an earplug in a small plastic bag taped to the antenna. No competition for X-Lax's huge boom box. And there was probably only one station around here—operated by the school.

Just as he was about to close the suitcase, Hector noticed something in one of the side pockets. He took out a small wooden frame holding an old photo—the only picture there was of the whole family together. He remembered the day his mother had made all of them, including Papá and Filiberto, don their Sunday best and go down to Fox Plaza, where there was a special on family portraits. Papá, his white hat in hand, stood in the back with Fili and Hector. Mamá and Aurora sat smiling in the front of the men, who looked as if they wished they were anyplace else.

Stuck to the back of the frame was a white envelope. For a moment he thought of last night, when he had found his mother sitting on her bed, letters spread around her.

"Mamá, what are you doing?"

"Recordando," Conchita answers.

"You want to be alone? I just came in to say good night."

"No, come sit down." She clears some space on the bed.

"What were you looking for, Mamá?" He glances at one of the papers. "This is Papá's writing."

"These are the letters he wrote to me when he first came to the States."

Hector wants to read one, but he's afraid to touch them, as if they will crumble in his hands. "There's so many."

"He was here for a year before I came over with baby Fili. He was so torn. First he wanted us to be together in the States. Then he dreamed of going back to Mexico. He wanted to buy us a little house outside of Chiapas."

Hector wonders how different their lives would have been there.

"But I wanted you to be born in the United States," she continues. "Even when you were a tiny baby inside me, I could feel that you were going to be someone special."

She lifts her hand, reaches out to touch his face, then brings it to her own cheek. In that second, he wants her to stop. There is no room inside him to store whatever she is about to tell him.

"When I was about four months pregnant with you, your father was away in Michigan, picking cherries. Fili and I were living in a shack over by Socorro, in back of a farm. It was horrible and dusty, and there was only a faucet out in the yard where we had to get water for the dishes and bathing and everything. While he was gone, I filled out the application for housing. I didn't tell him. He would have said no."

She closes her eyes as if she doesn't want to see the past. "When he came back I told him I wasn't going back to Mexico. I told him we could get the apartment if he had a steady job. I told him they were taking applications at Farah. That's how we ended up here."

Hector waits, hoping that's all his mother wanted to say.

But she goes on. "The day he was supposed to start at Farah, he got up and went. But that night was the first time he stayed out late. He came home drunk. I asked him to promise me he would never drink again, but he wouldn't. He said he didn't think he could work at that place and live here and not drink." Conchita wipes her eyes with the edge of her bedsheet.

"It's not your fault that he drank." Hector offers her a tissue from the box on her side table.

"I always felt like if I had said to him, 'Filemón, don't work there if you don't like it,' or if I had said to him that someday we would return to Chiapas, just given him some hope, he wouldn't have drunk. But he never stopped. He never forgave me for making him stay."

"No, Mamá, that's not true."

Conchita brushes off his words and looks at him fiercely. "Hector, when I saw the way you were growing up, the way you liked to read and the way you spoke English, I knew I had made the right decision."

The words hit Hector like punches.

"When I saw you up there helping Father Ochoa with the Mass day after day, I knew I had followed God's will."

Hector waits for her to say, *But now . . .*

"Things happened to make your life harder than it should be. Your brother, Fili, *que en paz descanse,* he was always restless. Never at peace. But you were always different. Even your father realized—"

Hector stands up abruptly and starts to leave, unable to hear any more.

"Promise me you will always be like that, so close to God. I won't mind your not being with us as long as I know that."

Hector turns and sees his reflection in the mirror over his mother's dresser. The small room, almost completely filled by the queen-size bed and ornate dresser, seems to be closing in on him.

"I have to go, Mamá," he says.

"Wait, wait," Conchita calls out. "Let me give you *la bendición.*"

Hector bends and drops his head limply while Conchita makes the sign of the cross on his forehead.

Hector held the envelope in his open palm, as though weighing it. No, he wouldn't open it yet. He didn't want to do anything that might starve or feed the flame flickering inside him. He placed the unopened envelope and family photograph in his bottom drawer, under the blue pajamas he would never wear.

5

"You know how to play chess?" Dr. Luna asked.

"Yes," Hector answered, wondering what that had to do with anything.

"I'll take whites," said Dr. Luna. The board was already set, with cheap plastic playing pieces, on a small table in the middle of the room.

Ten minutes went by without a word. The only sound an "mmm" from Dr. Luna when Hector's queen took his rook.

Just when Hector was beginning to feel relieved that the school psychologist was not going to ask him probing questions, Dr. Luna said: "So . . ."

Here we go, Hector thought.

"What's going on?" He didn't lift his eyes from the board.

Dr. Luna looked more like a mental patient than a doctor. With dark bags under his bloodshot eyes and yellow, tobacco-stained fingers, he looked as if he had spent the past twenty years locked up in a psych ward. No wonder X-Lax called him "The Lunatic." "Another Furman loser who can't get a job in the real world" was Hector's impression.

"Not a thing," Hector responded.

Dr. Luna slid a bishop diagonally across three squares, quickly, as if hoping that Hector wouldn't notice, as if his attempts at conversation were a simple diversionary tactic, to win the game.

"Your teachers say you're not doing your homework. You sit in class like a lump."

So that was it. Mrs. Pana had ratted on him.

"You don't play sports. You're not signing up for field trips. You don't hang out with anyone. Why?"

Hector moved his knight away from Dr. Luna's bishop. It was a stupid question that didn't deserve an answer. Why do work meant for fourth graders? Why hang out with people you don't like?

"I got your transcripts from Ysleta High. Good grades.

Excellent, actually." Dr. Luna nodded his head toward an open manila folder on his cluttered desk. "You're a good student."

Dr. Luna fiddled with his queen nervously, unsure about dashing into enemy territory to take Hector's knight. *Do it, pendejo*, Hector thought. *Then my rook will take your queen.*

But Dr. Luna recognized the trap and moved a pawn instead. He smiled as if to say, *I'm not as stupid as you think.* Then he sat back in his chair and consulted his watch. Hector heard another kid arrive outside, Dr. Luna's ten o'clock appointment.

"You need to participate," Dr. Luna said, finally looking up from the board. He was through playing games. "If you don't engage, you won't be able to stay here. You think this place is bad? You haven't been around. Wait and see."

When everything else fails, threaten, thought Hector. There was something liberating about Dr. Luna's finally getting down to basics.

Dr. Luna pushed back his chair and stood up. "I'll see you again next week. Do your homework. I want you to sign up for at least one extracurricular activity. I want to hear that you are doing something, even if you don't like it."

Hector got up to leave, and Dr. Luna took his arm. "If you don't participate, I'm saying, if you don't do the minimum, I will have to recommend that you be transferred to another facility."

There it was, straight out. Dr. Lunatic didn't even bother to hide his disgust. At least he and Hector had that much in common.

The Nortons (that's what the students called the Furman staff for reasons that no one remembered) were quick to prevent any type of grouping that could lead to gang formation. Black kids, white kids, Latino kids, and Native Americans were forced to mingle in the dorms and classrooms. Every week, new cafeteria seating assignments were posted. It didn't make for the most pleasant meals, but Colonel Chicken Wings wanted kids to sit with people they wouldn't necessarily choose.

Out on the basketball court, during one of the few hours when kids could do as they pleased, things were different. There, kids clumped together naturally along racial colors: white, brown, and black. The Chicano kids called themselves the "Carnales." They called the white team the "Gabachos" and the black team the "Mayates." The whole thing reminded Hector of the water molecules he had studied in chemistry class back at Ysleta High. When the heat was on, the molecules reluctantly separated; when the water cooled, they again sought their comfortable associations.

Hector walked over to the court, where the Carnales were warming up for a game against the Mayates. He sat down at a distance, his back against a lamppost with a light that never shone, because no one was allowed outside after dark. Some of the Carnales were trying to organize a standard two-line layup drill, but there was too much horsing around to get any kind of rhythm going. The kids on the rebound line pushed and poked one another as they bad-mouthed the players at the other end of the court. Of the eight Chicanos out there, only two seemed to be taking the drill seriously. A kid named Tulito waited for his turn to run a layup, jumping up and down, shaking his arms loosely by his side. Paco, the tallest of the bunch, shouted at the clowns on the rebound line to stop their farting around.

At six feet, Hector was as tall as Paco and probably as good a shooter as Tulito. If he walked over and asked to be let in, or if he just stood in the line and waited his turn for a layup, the Carnales would soon see that they could use someone like him. Back home Hector occasionally played one-on-one with his friend Sammy or five-on-five in gym class, but for him basketball's benefits were best achieved alone. In the evening, when there was only a half hour of light left in the day, he'd go to the deserted basketball court across from his house. There he'd lose himself in games he invented or just dribble and shoot unconsciously while he worked things out in his mind. Like on the evening before he left for Furman.

The projects' basketball court isn't lit, but in the moonlight he can see the dilapidated rim well enough. He likes using the court at this hour, when no one is around. He imagines that his skills are better in the dark. He has learned to depend more on instinct than on eyesight to find the basket.

He goes through his routine. Ten layups from the right side and then ten layups with the left hand. He moves to the invisible free throw line and shoots ten times from there. After this warm-up he begins to move around the perimeter, making jump shots from wherever he rebounds the ball. The sound of the ball bouncing on the concrete reminds him of a hand slapping a cheek. The basketball hits the backboard with a *twang* before it is swallowed by the chains dangling from the rim.

"You shouldn't be out here," a voice says.

He looks around to see Aurora, wearing the purple shorts and the Texas Cowboys T-shirt she wears to sleep.

"You're my mother now?"

"Have you forgotten that this is where it all started? It's not like the Discípulos don't ever come here."

Hector arches himself up in the air for a long fadeaway shot.

"You have a death wish or something?"

"After tonight you won't have to worry anymore. I'll be far, far away." Hector swivels away from her, slapping the ball with his open palm.

"It's good that you're getting away from this place," Aurora says, sounding older than her fourteen years.

"Yeah, your plan for my life will work out just fine," he says, punctuating each word with a bounce of the ball. Even as he says it, he feels a pang of remorse. This is not how he wants to spend the last night at home. He stops dribbling and walks over until he is close enough to see that she is biting her lip.

He knows what she's thinking. "You think it was my fault," he says accusingly.

"No, I already told you . . . Things just got out of control."

"Fili was the one out of control. Now I'm the one who has to pay for it."

"It's over now, and you can make a new start. You can still do all the things you wanted to do. Go to college—"

"I'm going to a fucking prison!"

40

"It's not a prison! You haven't even seen it, and you've already made up your mind. You've already given up. You owe it to—"

"I don't owe shit to anybody. I wish you'd get off my back. Live your own life."

"You *don't* owe me anything, Hector. I just meant that you owe it to yourself to not be like Dad or Fili. They didn't try. They just gave up."

"We can't all be perfect like you." He says these last words without anger. He's spent. He has a strong urge to stop talking, never to talk again.

"Let's go back in," says Aurora, unfazed.

"In a while," he responds, his words barely audible.

"Once you're out there, you can forget about this place. The Discípulos, everything. Even if none of this had happened, going to this school would still be a good thing for you."

"Well, then everything turned out for the best. Let's go in and tell Mamá. I'm sure the two of you will be very happy, living together in your fantasy world." He whirls around again, smacking the ball so hard the noise echoes off the nearby buildings.

When he turns back to where Aurora had been standing, all he sees is darkness.

———

"Hey!" Tulito's shout woke Hector from his stupor. Tulito was pointing at the beat-up brown ball rolling toward Hector's feet. Hector pulled in his legs before it could touch him. Then he stood up, looked at Tulito as if to say, *Get your own ball,* and walked away.

6

He didn't remember whether he had reacted outwardly to Dr. Luna's "requests" to do his homework and to sign up for at least one extracurricular activity. Maybe he just got up and left, or maybe he nodded slightly, an almost imperceptible, reluctant acquiescence. In any event, Hector started to do the assignments. It was as good a way as any to pass the time—though not much time. In half an hour he did what it took the others two hours to accomplish with difficulty.

The extracurricular activity was another matter. Hector studied the postings outside the entrance to the cafeteria. All of them involved doing things with others: talking, singing, acting, building, learning, playing either a sport or a musical instrument in a group.

At the bottom of the bulletin board, he saw a faded sheet describing various classes taught by inmates serving life sentences at a nearby state penitentiary. The inmates came to Furman every Sunday morning and met with students for a couple of hours. The classes included Bible study, bodybuilding, understanding and conquering addiction, and a shoot-the-bull discussion group about how to make it in the outside world after reform school. Hector wondered how a lifer would be qualified to teach that. The one that caught Hector's eyes was:

DUMBBELLS FOR THE MIND

Learn the ancient art of concentration. Strengthen the powers of the mind as you lift weights. Let the dumbbells make you smart.

He decided he would go to that one. How much group interaction could the ancient art of concentration require? The following Sunday, on a patch of shade cast by the side of the gym, he saw a few kids setting up dumbbells. Others were bringing folding chairs from the cafeteria. He was surprised to see X-Lax in the group.

"Hector the Erector!" X-Lax shouted when he saw Hector milling around. "You here for the dumbbells to make you smart? Get your sorry carc-ass over here!"

Hector regretted his decision already. How solitary an activity could lifting dumbbells be if X-Lax was in the group? Still, he kept ambling toward X-Lax and the other four students. "What are we supposed to do?" he asked.

"Lift, rest, jump, rest, lift, rest, jump, rest," X-Lax answered with a laugh. "It's perfect for you, man. You don't have to say a word."

When Hector first saw Díaz, the teacher, he was immediately disappointed. He had expected someone who looked like a killer. Instead, the guy who walked slowly toward them, dressed in a regulation blue prison jumpsuit, was smaller than Hector. He looked like Mr. Ortíz, Hector's English teacher back at Ysleta High, whom everyone suspected of being gay.

As Díaz approached, the kids formed a loose line. "What do I do?" Hector asked. Uncharacteristically, X-Lax simply lifted a finger to his lips. Hector moved next to X-Lax and waited.

Díaz stood in front of the six-man formation. He didn't acknowledge the new participant. Under his arm he carried something that looked like a map. In his right hand he held a roll of masking tape. The map turned out to be a diagram of the body's muscles. On the side of the gym, Díaz taped the sinewy, red figure of a skinless man, his green eyes popping like peeled grapes. Then he named each exercise and pointed to its corresponding muscle. "These are the places you should shine the flashlight when you do each routine. When you lift, feel the tension there. When you rest, feel the relaxation there. Okay."

Hector gathered that the "okay" was a signal that Díaz's lecture was over. The kids separated a few spaces from one another and began the weight-lifting routines. Some sat on chairs and curled. Others lay on the ground and pumped. One began by jumping rope with slow, looping swirls that barely cleared his feet. The whole thing reminded Hector of watching television with the sound off. He waited for Díaz to give him some instruction. But Díaz ignored him, left him standing there in awkwardness.

Hector moved to the side, picked up a dumbbell, and began to lift it quickly from his thigh to his chest. The dumbbell was light, ten pounds. He noticed that all of the weights were the same. This was easier than he'd imagined. Was this all he had to do to get Dr. Luna off his back?

When his right arm tired, he switched the dumbbell to his left hand and continued. Soon he tired of that. The whole thing was incredibly boring, pointless. Someone grabbed his arm, forced him to stop, the dumbbell halfway to his chest.

Díaz said nothing, just motioned with his finger, asking Hector to follow him. They stopped in front of a kid Hector had heard others call Sansón. "Watch him," said Díaz. "Then do what he does."

Sansón was lifting dumbbells from his shoulder to as far up as his arms could reach. His eyes were wide open and unblinking. His gaze went past Hector, as if Hector were invisible.

It was not the first time Hector had noticed Sansón. Once, in English class, when Mrs. Pana had asked Sansón to read aloud, Hector had observed his bulging, brown muscles and his face, round and rough, like a Toltec stone. The childish way he mouthed each syllable, the ignorant pauses in the middle of the simplest words, led Hector to believe that Sansón was as dumb as he was strong.

Now here he was, an example for Hector. An example of what? Concentration? *Maybe it's easier when you're an imbecile,* Hector thought.

"Watch how he breathes," said Díaz. "Watch his nostrils."

Hector focused in. Sansón's nostrils flared with inhaled breath as the weight went up, closed slightly as he exhaled and the weight went down. It was all one movement, the breathing in and lifting up, the breathing out and lifting down.

"Now you do it, Hector," said Díaz.

That night, tossing and turning in his top bunk, Hector wondered how Díaz had known his name. The lights had been off for hours, it seemed. From the sounds below, Hector guessed that X-Lax was also unable to sleep.

"Hector? Are you awake?"

Hector's first instinct was to freeze. He knew that if he answered X-Lax's question, it would be a green light for a long discourse of the X-Lax variety. Then again, that was better than facing a long, sleepless night. Recklessly perhaps, Hector plunged ahead. "Yeah."

"I can't sleep, man. I swear, I get insomnia every Sunday night. I kid you not. I think it's the weight lifting. It's that flashlight that Díaz talks about. It's too bright, man."

"Flashlight?" Hector repeated.

"It gets turned on during the dumbbells, and then it keeps on shining. I'm telling you, man, the worst thing about this place is when the lights go off. Then you're left with the flashlight. Know what I'm saying? I mean, if it's not remembering something bad that happened to you, then it's dreaming about something good you don't have and can't get. Either way, the stuff comes at you something fierce. I guess it must mean that the dumbbells are working and all, but who needs all that remembering and missing?"

"Why do you do the dumbbells, then?" Hector wondered if his question was loud enough for X-Lax to hear. Regardless, X-Lax went rambling on.

"It's like a conveyor belt inside there, like in a factory. The conveyor belts just keep coming around and around, bringing the same old shit. And you sit there with your light on, sniffing it. Shit!"

An image of his father at the factory came to Hector. The little electric scissors that hung from the ceiling on a curled cord, the stack of cloth that needed to be patterned and cut.

"I told Díaz once that I didn't think the dumbbells were for me. I told him that things inside my head were more mixed up than ever. He said things always got worse before they got better. He said that was a good sign. That I was going on to the next step, from shining the flashlight on the muscles to shining the light on the garbage inside my head. But I ask you, Hector Erector, what's the point? What's the point of sniffing the turds on the conveyor belt? The turds don't bother me during the daytime when there's all kinds of stuff to do. Even in this place. Listen, man, I'm baring my insides to you here, but I don't want you letting people know about my intimate secrets, you hear?"

"No."

"Hell, I ain't worried about you telling anybody. How many words have you said since you've been here—three? Guess us handy-dandy handicaps got to stick together. You with one ear and me with one ball. Hey, I wonder if the fact that you have one ear makes you better at hearing, the way that my one ball makes me better at loving and roving? Where was I, anyway?"

"The turds."

"Oh, yeah. You want to know what turd was going around the conveyor belt tonight?"

Silence.

"Okay, I'll tell you. It was about this foster mother I had. Her name was Mrs. Johnson. She was a white lady, which was unusual, 'cause most of the foster homes I've been in were run by black folks, probably on account of they needed the money, and most of them don't mind having a bunch of kids around. But this lady, Mrs. Johnson, I was the first foster kid she ever took in. And you could tell she wasn't doing it for the money but because she needed to take care of someone, to feel useful or religious or whatever. She lived in this little house with a cement porch, and the kitchen was clean and I had my own room. When I got there, man, I thought I finally died and went to heaven. Nice lady. I was twelve or so, and all I had to do to have all the comforts—I'm talking snacks at any time, whenever,

TV in my room, the whole thing—all I had to do was let the old woman take care of me. Man, that's the kind of setup foster kids salivate about."

X-Lax stopped talking. Hector turned on his side, his good ear upward. There was no sound or movement coming from the bunk below. "X-Lax, you asleep?" he whispered.

"Naah." It was a delayed response.

"What happened with the old lady?" Hector tried not to sound interested.

"Eh? What happened? The usual. One day I packed a whole bunch of her stuff into her Fairlane and took off. What else was going to happen? You wanna know what turd was on the conveyor belt tonight? It was the old lady's face. She had this way of opening her eyes and mouth, you know, like when you're pretending to be surprised. Shit! I wish I had a few beers. I don't even feel like whacking off. I must be sick. Hell, I'd settle for some cough syrup right now.

"Hey, Hector, what's on your conveyor belt?"

"Nothing. Factory's on strike." But it wasn't true.

7

At the end of class, Mr. Ortíz, his English teacher, asks him to wait a minute, hands him a paper. "I want to give you this. It's about a contest the Lions Club has every year, for all the ninth graders in El Paso. It's an essay contest. This year's theme is 'America—the Pursuit of Happiness.' Do you know where that phrase comes from, *the pursuit of happiness?*"

Hector says the first thing that comes to mind. "The Declaration of Independence."

"Correct," he says. "Anyway, I thought you might want to give it a shot. You're the best writer we have. If anyone can win it for us, you can. They want three typewritten pages by next week."

"Is that all?" Hector has heard things about Mr. Ortíz and worries that he might put a move on him.

"Yes," Mr. Ortíz says softly, "that's all."

Hector decides to write the thing, almost as a joke. He doesn't think he'll ever show it to anyone. Only Aurora—he pays her five bucks to write it with a calligraphy pen so it looks like it's typed, since they don't have a typewriter or computer. She's good with her hands that way. His father calls her La Mayita because, according to him, she carries the Maya's art in her blood.

Hector finds a quote in a book of famous sayings: *Happiness is the fulfillment of duty.* When he reads the quote, by a man named Immanuel Kant, he thinks of his father going to work at the pants factory day after day. Hector writes about him coming over from Chiapas when he was a young man. He writes about him working in the cotton fields of Texas, in the lettuce fields of the Río Grande Valley, in the potato fields of Alabama, and in the cherry orchards of Michigan until Mamá found him that steady job. Hector visited him at the factory once. Papá had to work fast because he had to put out a quota of pants, every hour, every day, every week. Some days he came home with his fingers all cut up. Out the window of his room, Hector had seen him stick his hands deep in the mud of that patch of ground he called his garden, like it was some kind of medicine.

So Hector writes about how for his father the pursuit of happiness is the fulfillment of his duty. That's what the signers of the Declaration of Independence meant when they said that man had certain rights. The right to pursue happiness is the opportunity to do what needs to be done so that others can have what they need, and there's no way to be happy unless this duty is fulfilled.

The funny thing is that even though the paper's about happiness, Hector feels sad. He thinks of his father and how he never hears him laugh. It's confusing. The more he writes, the crappier he feels. Impulsively, he sticks the paper in an envelope after Aurora finishes printing it, and he sends it off. He doesn't even keep a copy of it.

A month later, Mr. Ortíz tells him he won first place. The Lions Club is having an awards ceremony next Wednesday, during their weekly luncheon meeting. The first-, second-, and third-place winners will read their papers and get their awards. He's supposed to bring his family. It's important that they be there.

Wait. Hold on. His father works. He only gets an hour off for lunch. His mother works, too. She may be able to get off. But there's no way his father can go. And his brother won't be able to go either. Mr. Ortíz looks at him funny. Like he doesn't believe him. "Are you sure your father can't get an extra hour off from work? The essay, after all, is about him."

Papá's English is not too good. The thought of him there, perhaps wearing the Mexican straw hat he saves for special occasions, scares Hector. And Filiberto—what if he comes and picks a fight with a Lion for some reason? It could happen.

"I'll mention it to them," Hector tells Mr. Ortíz.

"You should be proud," he says. "That essay came from the heart. That's why it won."

"Yeah," Hector says. He starts walking before Mr. Ortíz can say anything else. Actually that essay is not from the heart. If it had been from the heart, he would have said that the pursuit of happiness is so much bullshit. Who's happy? His father? Mr. Ortíz? Why does happiness even matter? That's what Hector thinks. And there's no way he's going to tell anyone in his family about this thing. Everyone is too busy. They have to make a living.

So Wednesday comes, and around eleven Hector gets excused from social studies. He goes to the bathroom and puts on a white shirt and a clip-on tie that he borrowed from Frank, the manager at the Piggly Wiggly, where he works after school. Then he goes out to the parking lot to wait for Mr. Ortíz to pick him up. It *is* too bad his parents couldn't make it. They just couldn't get out of work. They were very sorry. Mr. Ortíz gives him this look like he knows he's lying. What's he going to do? It's better this way.

During lunch Hector notices that everyone puts their white napkins on their lap, so he does the same. Two tables over, he sees a kid in a dark blue suit, his hair, wet with sweat, still in perfect place. At the table next to him sits a girl with thick, goofy glasses. He figures they're the second- and third-place winners. The boy with the wet hair is sitting next to a woman in a flowered dress. It's the boy's mother, Hector's sure. The father is on the boy's other side. Next to the father sits an older woman who's a grayer version of the mother. The kid even brought his grandmother.

He thinks about what it would have been like to have his family with him. His father probably wouldn't have known that after you cut a piece of meat, you switch the fork over to your right hand again. His mother would have worn that bright yellow polyester outfit she takes to church every Sunday. She would have told everyone that she works as a cook at the Mt. Carmel parochial school. Filiberto would have fallen asleep at the table, or said something nasty to one of the Lions. Aurora, on the other hand, she would've had fun. She gets a big kick out of everything.

Someone's clinking a glass. The clinking continues until

everyone hushes. The head Lion gets up and introduces the third-place winner. Hector looks toward the girl, expecting her to get up, but instead it's the boy with the wet hair who gets up.

Hector tries hard to listen to the boy read his essay, but he can't concentrate on what he's saying. He hears only phrases and words. Land of opportunity. Dreams. Lots of stuff about dreams. He's a real professional actor, this kid. He moves his hands. Whenever he says "dream," he taps his heart in exactly the same way, with his fist closed. It looks like he has his essay memorized.

Then it's the girl's turn. Her first name is Sonya. The Lion who introduces her has trouble pronouncing her last name. When she gets up there, the girl closes her eyes for a couple of seconds, as if trying to remember something. Then she opens her eyes and looks straight at her mother, who is almost, but not quite, smiling. The girl starts speaking slowly, calmly. Like she doesn't care about what anybody thinks, like she's reading for someone who could listen to her forever.

The intelligence of her writing comes across like a ray of sunlight. God has given human beings the tools necessary to pursue happiness. He has made us in such a way that in the honest search for happiness we ultimately end up searching for Him. Not all countries allow persons to do this.

Some places impose a way of life on people, presume to know what happiness consists of, and do not trust their citizens to find out for themselves. Her family is from Russia. They are Jewish. In Russia, they were not allowed to practice their religion, to seek God openly, to pursue the one and only path they felt would make them happy. Her father was imprisoned for his pursuit. He died in prison.

Hector listens to every single word, dazed by the discovery that such thoughts could be generated by this person who seems so . . . so . . . out of place. There's stuff going on behind that painfully shy face of hers; there's courage behind those goofy glasses. She's not making it up. She's not trying to impress anyone. She's talking about things she would willingly die for. It shouldn't be so surprising that there are kids his age who think about these things, but it is. So surprising that he forgets he is next until he hears his name over the microphone.

He feels calm on the way up there. He unfolds his paper and reads loudly and with conviction, the way Mr. Ortíz told him to. Then, when he gets to the part about what life was like for his father when he was a farmer in Chiapas, he looks up and sees the empty chair where his father would have sat had he come, had Hector told him about the luncheon, had Hector not been ashamed of him, and something like a ball of fire rushes up from his stomach and settles in his throat. He stops talking. He waits for it to go down again. Only it doesn't go away. And now the fire turns into a hot liquid that starts gushing out of his eyes and his nose. The paper in front of him is trembling. It's getting wet with drops of snot and tears. He tries to continue reading, but he can't, because the moment he opens his mouth something that sounds like a sob comes out, and he knows there are a thousand of them just sitting there, waiting to fly out as soon as he opens his mouth, like bats out of a cave.

The Lion man gets up and pats him in the back. Mr. Ortíz stands up and makes his way up toward him. Hector stares at his father's empty chair until he can't see it anymore because he's shaking and heaving and the head Lion is telling folks to "give us a moment, please," and Mr. Ortíz is taking him outside through a side door.

"You all right, son?" Mr. Ortíz asks. He has his arm tightly around Hector's shoulder. "That's okay. Let it out. Let it all out," he says. "It's good for you."

"I didn't tell my parents," Hector says, when he is able to talk, "about the luncheon."

"I know," Mr. Ortíz says. "I know you didn't."

"I'd like to go home now."

"We can go back in. You can finish your speech. But we can also go home, if you like."

Hector closes his eyes and all he can think about is the

girl with the goofy glasses. How she should have won first place, how much courage she had to say what she said. And it isn't just fear, really, that keeps him from going back, that makes him start walking toward Mr. Ortíz's car. It's something else. It's like being alone and wishing there was someone, anyone, there with you. It's something overwhelmingly lonesome and sad. Something he knew was there, but never felt before.

Hector sat at his desk in his Furman cell, staring at a blank piece of notebook paper. The essay on the causes of the Civil War, the one that was supposed to be only a page long, the one that he thought he could polish off in ten minutes tops, had already taken him more than an hour, and he had yet to write the first word. He heard a knock. Sansón stood at the doorway, grinning, like he was afraid to ask for something.

"*Ése,*" said Sansón, "where you learn to read like that?"

"What?" Hector touched his ear, searching for the hearing aid that wasn't there.

"That was good this morning. The old man pulling the tuna." Sansón grimaced as he pulled hard on an invisible fishing line.

The Old Man and the Sea, Hector guessed at the charade. In English class that morning Mrs. Pana had asked Hector to read aloud.

"Where you learn to read like that, *ése?*" Sansón repeated his question.

He has the mind of a six-year-old, Hector thought. "At school."

"Shhh . . . I wish I could read like that."

"It takes practice."

"Is that something you can teach someone? To read like that?"

First you'd have to get a brain, Hector said to himself. "All you have to do is practice."

"I read all the time. My brother sends me magazines about cars. I read the words, but it takes too long for them to make sense. By the time I get to the last word, I forgot what the first word was." Sansón giggled.

"It will come." Hector looked at the blank piece of paper in front of him, hoping Sansón would see that he was busy and move along.

"This morning in class, *ése,* when you were reading, it made sense in my mind. I saw the old man pulling the tuna."

"Yeah?" Hector tried to remember whether Hemingway had called the fish a tuna.

"I'm only in that class because Mrs. Pana, she lets me. I'm in VOC training—you know, shop. I'm training to be an automotive technician. Mrs. Pana said I could sit in her class. I'm trying to pick up on my reading."

"Why?" Hector thought out loud.

It didn't seem like an unusual or disparaging question to Sansón. "I don't know. At first I wanted to learn because I sound like a *sonso* every time I read." Sansón waited for Hector to agree, but Hector held his lips tight. "Then I wanted to learn in case I need to for work. Like if I have to read the specs on a car I'm fixing, *verdá*?" Hector nodded. "Now I just wanna be able to see the pictures you get when you read."

"Like in the movies," Hector pointed out.

"Simón, ése, como en las vistas."

Hector began to write on the top margin of the paper: *The Causes of the Civil War.* He wrote slowly, squinting as if in deep concentration. It wasn't working. Sansón still stood in the doorway. Hector heard him scratch his head. When Hector looked up again, Sansón had the same grin, like someone who wants to borrow money, but is too timid to ask.

"I could practice reading with you." Hector was surprised to hear the words come out of his mouth.

"De veras, ése? Are you sure?"

Hector hesitated. He wondered if there was a way to pull the words back from the air, where they still floated. "Yeah," he said. He was sure Sansón wouldn't detect his tone of regret.

"*Mañana?*"

"Okay."

"What time, *ése?*"

"This time, I guess."

"We can do it in the study room."

"All right. Wherever."

Sansón remained, perhaps to make sure Hector didn't change his mind. "Can we read that book about the old man and the tuna?"

Hector nodded, and finally, Sansón disappeared. Hector was still wondering what the hell had just happened when Sansón's head appeared again in the doorway. "Thanks, *ése*," he said. Then he waved his giant hand the way a two-year-old waves bye-bye.

Hector sat there with his paper, mystified by what he had done. The thought of picking up a book, any book, and reading it for any reason other than because he had to was bad enough. The thought of listening to Sansón "read" was going to be Chinese torture. The best he could come up with was the thought he'd had when he watched Sansón lift the dumbbells: Sansón reminded him of someone, but he could not remember who.

8

From then on, like clockwork, Sansón showed up at Hector's door every night, toting a book or an automotive magazine. Hector let him read for a few minutes, then took the book or magazine out of his hand and read it aloud for the remaining half hour. Hector didn't hide the fact that he considered it a chore—but Sansón didn't notice. Hector read at his own speed, not waiting for Sansón to keep up. That was the way one learned to read. Whenever Sansón asked about the meaning of a story, Hector shrugged him off. That was also the way you learned to read, by listening and not asking questions. There was no need to make more out of this. And besides, discussing the meaning of stories made Hector feel nauseous.

From then on, every day after classes were over, Sansón tugged Hector to the side of the gym to lift weights and skip rope with him. "Come on, *ése*," Sansón had urged him the first time. Once Hector gave in, there was no going back. "Breathe in when you lift up, breathe out when you let the dumbbell down. Slowly." Teaching Hector how to lift was Sansón's way of repaying the favor.

One day, as they were putting the dumbbells away, Tulito came up to them.

"Big guy," he said to Sansón, "we need you out on the court."

"*No puedo, ése.* I got outside detail today."

"Man, it's a game against the Gabachos. We need some muscle in the middle."

"What you want me for? I can't shoot."

"I'll shoot, *ése*. All you have to do is put your *culo* in front of Curly, and block him out so he can't get the rebound, in case I ever miss. Not that I will."

"I can't. If I miss outside detail, they won't keep me on the list."

"What's more important, *ése?* Helping your *carnales*, or picking up beer cans?"

"*No sé.* " Sansón was struggling with the question. Then

his face lit up. "Why don't you take Hector here?"

There was an embarrassing moment when Tulito looked Hector up and down, measuring whether he would do.

"Not me," said Hector. He folded up the cafeteria chair.

Tulito turned to Sansón. Dismissively, he said, "We need a *carnal,* man."

The insult felt like a wasp sting.

"Take Hector," Sansón said. It was an order this time. There was a different look on Sansón's face, more grown-up.

"Come on." Tulito started walking toward the court. He didn't turn around to see if Hector followed.

"I'll take the chair in," Sansón said to Hector. "Go." On his face, the same look of child turned man.

The Carnales had seven players warming up on the court. When Tulito arrived, three of the players moved to the sidelines. Hector slowed, his legs suddenly heavy. "You playing?" asked one of the kids on the sidelines. Hector shrugged.

The referee—a black kid, chosen by the white kids and the Chicano kids because he was presumed to be impartial—blew a whistle. "Let's get this show on the road!" he yelled.

The Carnales huddled. Paco, the tall one, spoke. "We'll start the usual. You," he said to Hector, "keep your eye on Curly, the center. He likes to back into the basket, then hook the ball off the backboard. All you have to do is keep him from pushing you out. Stay on his ass. When we got the ball, keep him away from the basket so someone else can rebound." There were snorts and giggles all around. *Good luck to you, sucker,* Hector took them to mean. "I'm going to start at center," continued Paco, "but when you come in, Chato here will come out. I'll move to forward, and you'll take center. All right, everybody move the ball around. Let's tire them out. Don't anybody try the fancy shit. Okay, let's go!"

These guys think this game is real, thought Hector with a smile. The court was crowded with onlookers. X-Lax, over on the Gabacho side, caught Hector's eye and began to pump his pelvis while pointing at the Carnales.

The referee was useless. He blew the whistle unnecessarily when someone scored. Otherwise he ran from side to side, turning a blind eye to the pushing and shoving and pawing that went on. Hector watched Curly, the boy he was to guard, if he ever went in. Curly was only a head taller than Hector but broad. By the looks of him, the word *juvenile* did not apply, but the word *delinquent* did. No wonder Tulito had gone looking for Sansón.

Hector waited to go in, feeling more and more restless as the minutes passed and substitutions were made. An energy cranked up inside of him, like electricity building up in a wire, waiting to light something up, to make something churn.

When he finally went in, he knew just what to do. He was there not to play but to work. He hooked on to Curly like a lover, whether Curly had the ball or not. He was close enough to taste the kid's sweat—acrid and sweet, like the Pine-Sol Mamá used to clean the toilet. *They want a burro, not a horse,* Hector thought. Stubbornly he shadowed his mark. Curly had trouble stretching his arms to catch the ball. He had trouble moving past Hector's hips. He couldn't back into the basket. He stopped looking for the ball, preoccupied with swatting Hector's hands from his chest, his arms, his back. He bumped his chest angrily against Hector. *You're getting pissed,* pendejo.

Hector kept on, his eyes on Curly, his mind aware of everyone else's moves. Even when the Carnales had the ball, he looked only to place his body between Curly and the basket. Tulito shot from the perimeter. The ball hit the rim and bounced toward Hector, who was underneath and in front of Curly's outstretched arms. Hector snatched the ball and bent forward quickly, his butt jutting into Curly's groin. Just as he passed the ball to Paco, Hector felt a burning slap on the back of his head. Curly's white face was flushed, fiery pink.

For a few seconds all eyes were on Hector and Curly

glaring at each other. Then Hector pushed Curly's chest away with his two hands. The gesture was forceful yet playful. *Come on,* it said, *let's get on with the game. It's nothing personal.* At that moment the confrontation dissolved, the ball bounced, and the players sprinted to the other side of the court.

The Carnales lost, but maybe not by as much as they would have had Curly been allowed to rebound, to make his sweet hook shot unimpeded. Hector had done what he was supposed to do. He started to walk off toward his dorm, but Curly stopped him.

Curly raised his hand, and, instinctively, Hector drew back. But Curly only wanted to touch fists. Though the gesture was delivered grudgingly, it was typical after-game protocol.

Hector did his duty, then continued on his way. "Hey," Tulito called after him. Hector stopped without turning around.

"Practice at four-thirty tomorrow." Hector heard Tulito say.

Hector's first impulse was to turn around and say: Órale, *I'll be there.* Instead, he shrugged his shoulders and turned his hands up, as if to say, *Who knows what tomorrow will bring?*

X-Lax caught up to him before Hector reached the entrance to the dorm.

"Hector, Hector, Hector," X-Lax said, putting his arm around Hector's shoulder. "I finally figured out what to call you." Hector shook off X-Lax's arm. "You are Clinto Estemadera. The Mexican version of Clint, my buddy Eastwood, man of few words, but burning inside. I hereby baptize you Clinto Estemadera, in the name of the Father, the Son, and the Holy Tamale."

9

There were only two ways to escape the Furman confines: go on a field trip or do outside detail. Earning the right to outside detail was not easy. It meant that the Nortons trusted you enough not to take off on a sprint the minute you smelled freedom. Picking up garbage or mowing the sloppy grass banks adjoining Interstate 10 under the sweltering San Antonio sun were, in the twisted world of Furman, privy-leges that only a chosen few could enjoy. It was back-breaking unpaid labor, but everyone wanted to do it.

"It's the only way to get a glimpse of life female," was

X-Lax's explanation of why he'd signed up. Not that he was ever picked. The Nortons correctly surmised that he was not the type who could handle liberty with serenity.

Hector never knew who put his name on the list, although he had a strong suspicion. One Saturday morning Sansón poked his head into Hector's room and told him to hurry up, the van was waiting. "Waiting for what?" Hector asked.

"*Pos para ir a trabajar,*" Sansón responded innocently.

The van, a beat-up, light-blue thing that looked as if it had been through World War II, took its load of slave labor to the outskirts of San Antonio, where folks liked to dump McDonald's refuse and empty cans of Coors. Hector was handed an old ski pole for picking up the garbage and a duffel bag, air-force issue, to put it in.

They spread out across the median that separated Interstate 10 East from West. Now and then a driver would honk, or some teenager would stick his head out of a whizzing vehicle and jeer. Who cared? The outside-detail gang was outside, walking ankle-high in dandelions and bluebonnets on a road that stretched all the way to California one way and to Maine the other.

The wildflowers reminded Hector of Papá's garden. It had been nothing more than a three-foot-wide trench that went around their apartment like a moat. In that space he crammed chili peppers: tiny red *piquins* that burned Hector's nose just by looking at them, and yellow and green *habaneros* that looked like Christmas-tree lights. Papá also planted cilantro, mint, parsley, tomato plants, and a peach tree that gave the same five pale pieces of fruit every year.

Then there were underground mysteries, such as carrots and onions that only Papá knew about. One year he even got a few stalks of corn to grow. There was no sense or order to the garden, as far as Hector could see. Colorful things were judged to be weeds and pulled; ugly things were pampered.

Papá's helper in the garden was Aurora. Papá taught her to plant in the early summer when the moon was full. He showed her how to save the seeds from the best chilies and how to replant them. She learned that female trees needed to be placed close to male trees so they would bear fruit. She knew when to prune, and she could tell the difference between a weed and a young tomato plant.

The one thing she couldn't do was carry water from the levy the way Papá could. He claimed that the water from the Río Grande, six blocks away, had a muddy richness the plants craved. He'd fill two white buckets and balance them on either end of a shovel he carried across his shoulders.

Aurora tried to imitate him. She'd walk with him to the ditch and come back sloshing a beach pail full of brown water. By the time she reached the garden, the water was always gone.

"*Mierda!*" she'd say. Papá had taught her to swear, too. She was the only one in the family allowed to curse. Even Mamá couldn't hide a fledgling smile when Aurora did it.

Where was he when Papá cared for his garden? Why was it that no one in the family laughed the few times Hector swore? The tall grass, the swaying blue flowers, the smells in the open air, pierced him with their unanswerable questions. Everything reminded him of time lost, of gifts not accepted when they were offered.

Hector stumbled on a rock.

"Watch yourself," said Sansón, bringing Hector back to the moment. "*Aguas con las* rattlesnakes."

"There's rattlesnakes?" Hector asked.

"The place's crawling with them," Sansón said.

Hector eyed him for a second. Not in a million years would he ever be able to tell if Sansón was pulling his leg.

"You're kidding me, right?" he finally asked.

"*Qué no, ése.* If you don't stop daydreaming, you'll step on their *cola.*"

"Don't they rattle first?"

"Only if you hear them," responded Sansón, trying not to laugh.

"Ha ha, very funny," said Hector. Nevertheless, he decided to keep his eyes on the ground and his ears open.

10

Hector dropped the rope and sank to the ground. That morning Díaz had instructed the group to increase their rope jumping to three five-minute sets with a one-minute break in between. Hector was in the middle of the third set when his legs filled with lead and there was no more air to suck. Díaz came over to where he sat and made him stretch out on the ground. He then lifted Hector's legs as far up as they would go.

"Owww," grunted Hector.

"Let's move to the shade," said Díaz. He pulled Hector up and helped him hobble to the side of the gym.

"My legs gave out," Hector said.

"I see," said Díaz, no sympathy in his voice.

They both looked over at Sansón's massive body skipping rope as lightly as a little girl.

"Maybe I'm not doing it right," Hector volunteered.

Still looking at Sansón, Díaz responded, "When I was a kid growing up in Mexico, we used to sing little songs when we skipped rope. I remember one that goes: *'Tin Marín de don pingué, cucara macara, titere fué, yo no fui, fue teté, pegalé a ella que ella fué.'* You ever hear that one?"

"My father used to say that to me and my sister when he was trying to decide whose turn it was to go to the store and get him a pack of cigarettes."

"Yeah. There's a whole bunch of other rhymes we used to sing that I don't remember anymore. There was one about a Doña Blanca and one about Los Maderos de San Juan. Or maybe it's the same one. I don't know. It's been so long."

The way Díaz said "so long" made Hector turn to look at him. He was surprised to hear emotion in Díaz's voice.

Díaz went on. "I remember one little girl who lived next to our house. Her name was Candelaria, but we called her Cande. She could jump rope for hours without missing a beat, one song after another."

In the silence that followed, Hector felt like asking Díaz

what he had done to get life in prison. Instead he said, "What's the point?"

Díaz did not seem to hear him. "It's amazing how much exercise little children do without minding it, or even realizing it—never getting tired, just playing one long game."

I'm not a child, Hector said to himself.

"Of course," said Díaz, as if responding to Hector's thoughts, "we're not children. But we can still be *like* children."

"You want me to sing?"

"Sure, if it will help you pace yourself, if it'll help you find a rhythm you're comfortable with, why not?"

"I thought we were supposed to train our minds. I don't get it," said Hector skeptically.

"There's no need to 'get' anything," Díaz said, without reproach. "You don't have to understand how the process works in order for it to work."

"But I need to know why we're doing what we're doing. I'm not Sansón. I have a brain." Hector grimaced a little at his own words.

"Look at him." Díaz pointed at Sansón with his chin. "There's nothing he wouldn't give to have your brain, as you say. But he can't. No matter how hard he tries, he will never have what you have. But you, you're fortunate—you can have what he has."

"What is that?" asked Hector.

"Oh, there's different words for it. Sometimes words get in the way, prevent you from seeing what they stand for. It's better if you try to discover for yourself what it is."

"Courage?" asked Hector. It was the first thing that came to mind.

Díaz shrugged. "And what is that? It's just a word, unless you're able to see in your mind a concrete example."

Hector saw Sansón hovering in the doorway of his room, angling for Hector to help him with his reading.

Díaz allowed him to dwell on that mental image for a few moments before he spoke again. "Start small. Before you tackle big things like courage, just try to jump rope like he does, with the unhurried but steady rhythm of a child playing a game. Or lift dumbbells like he does, slowly, breathing in and out, enjoying the way the different muscles feel. The rest will take care of itself."

As they sat there in a patch of shade, their backs against the gym, Hector felt a rare peace, like the time he and his father had sat together in their backyard, wordlessly watching a gliding hawk. Then Díaz stood up and left Hector to the solace of his own silence.

11

Something told Hector that the new kid didn't belong. Most kids look scared when they get to Furman, even though they try not to show it. You can tell by the hurried way they walk, or the way they keep their eyes down, darting here and there when they think no one is looking. But this kid walked slowly, head up and eyes taking it all in, as if he was looking for someone.

Hector watched the boy strut confidently across the yard with a soiled bag slung over his shoulder. That was another sign. Kids who have never been in a reform school try to bring as much junk as possible. Hector could tell by the shape of this kid's bag that it didn't contain much. Maybe he wasn't planning to stay long.

The next day Hector was standing in the cafeteria line when he had a strange sensation. He turned around and saw the new kid, who went by the name El Topo, looking directly at him. El Topo didn't avert his eyes when Hector caught his stare. Even from a distance Hector could make out a smirk on his thick lips. Hector held his gaze for a few seconds before turning back to the food servers.

Hector remembered the day when X-Lax had explained the Furman code regarding staring.

"There are lots of things you need to know to survive in this environment, Clinto," X-Lax expounded. "You're lucky you have me around. Now listen. If someone's looking at you, and you move your eyes like this"—he darted his eyeballs quickly to one side—"you send a signal that you are a pussy. But if you let your eyes linger on his for a second or two"—X-Lax looked into Hector's eyes, then nonchalantly looked away—"you're saying you don't want any trouble but you're not afraid either. You will not let yourself be ass-whipped without a fight. These are the kind of things you need to know, Clinto. It's not like they come naturally, know what I'm saying? Now if you catch someone staring at your buns, well, hell, that's another story."

El Topo's stare became a fact of life for Hector. It arrived that day in the cafeteria and never left. There was no mistaking the way El Topo hunted him as Hector walked out of the Sunday lecture, did his morning calisthenics, and waited for the van to take him to outside detail. There was something loud about El Topo's mute glare, a wordless violation.

One afternoon, when Hector was playing basketball with the Carnales against the Mayates, El Topo stood on the sidelines, following every move Hector made. One of the Mayate players left the court and El Topo substituted for him. The players and spectators stopped to take it in. El Topo, a Chicano, was playing on the black team. It wasn't a big enough deal to stop the game or even make an issue out of. It just struck everyone as weird.

El Topo came in for the player guarding Hector. He crouched defensively, attempting to restrict Hector's movement, and kept his eyes locked on Hector's face. Hector knew El Topo was not there to play a game.

Hector stayed cool. He soon learned that he was in much better shape than El Topo, and he used that to his advantage, darting around the blacktop in a deliberate effort to tire him. El Topo had trouble keeping up, partially because he had no peripheral vision. He stayed focused only on Hector. It was easy to outplay someone whose mind wasn't on the game.

Hector got the ball on top of the key. He nodded at Paco, and Paco set a pick for him. El Topo, trailing Hector like a hound dog, bounced off the pick and landed on his butt. Hector breezed through and scored. People chuckled as they ran back to the opposite basket, even the kids on El Topo's team. El Topo picked himself up and walked coolly toward Hector. With a frozen grin, he resumed guarding Hector, even though his team had the ball. Hector could see that behind the fake smile, El Topo was addled, so angry he didn't know which way was up.

One of the Mayates shot from beyond the imaginary three-point line. Hector sidestepped El Topo, rebounded easily, and passed to Tulito, who started to fast-break even before the ball was firmly in his grasp. Tulito bounced it a couple of times and banked it in the basket. No one was even close to him. The Mayates were going to lose the game because they'd let El Topo play. Whatever El Topo had done to get in the game was not worth the price.

Hector danced around El Topo, moving solely for the sake of moving. Though everything was happening fast, nothing was hurried. It was like one of those rare moments Díaz talked about in mind-training class, when everything slows down and thought becomes simply the force that moves the muscles. When Hector jumped, he felt like an astronaut bounding on the surface of the moon. The ball seemed to bounce even before it touched the ground, then it floated toward him like a giant, orange sun. He saw the open basket as if he were hovering over it.

Somewhere in front of Hector, like an annoying insect, a sweaty person tried to block his flow and anchor his flight, but he could not reach Hector. El Topo's anger bounced off an invisible shield. Hector got a pass with his back to the basket. In one motion he turned around and rose up, far beyond El Topo's outstretched arms, and with his fingertips spun the ball into the blue sky, toward the net.

El Topo didn't turn around to see the ball go in the basket. He bent over, chest heaving, and raised his hand, asking to be let out of the game. Hector was sorry to see him go. It was fun to play against an angry person. In fact, it was a shame that El Topo didn't lose it completely and explode with violence in front of everyone. Hector had won this small battle, but El Topo's humiliation was going to make the war ahead much harder. And now Hector knew that El Topo had some smarts. He had controlled himself enough to get out of the game before anyone learned his intent. Now Hector—and only Hector—knew why El Topo was at Furman.

12

Aurora:

I need you to do some things for me. In my desk drawer there's a Band-Aid box. Inside there's a medal of the Virgen—ask Mrs. Garza to send it to me. There's also a bankbook. Fili gave it to me the night he died. Papá started a savings account, and Fili added to it. The money is for you and Mamá now. Talk to Mrs. Garza about how to get it signed over.

I know what you're thinking, that it was for college, but things have changed. I'm not going to need it, but you and Mamá do. I'm counting on you to convince Mamá that this needs to be done. Es urgente. *Don't let her be a martyr. It's selfish to be a martyr. Especially the way things are now. Do it for Papá and Fili, if nothing else.*

Tu hermano,
Hector

BOOK two

1

Hector sat at the kitchen table pondering a physics word problem. Filiberto lay on the sofa, watching television. They both looked up when they heard the screen door slam. Aurora burst into the apartment.

"What happened?" asked Hector.

"Nooothing!" Aurora yelled on the way to her room.

"Tell me!" he shouted.

Hector got up with a sigh. Fili put his face down on the sofa cushion. On the TV screen a cheetah sprang from behind tall grass and began chasing a gazelle.

Hector stood in front of Aurora's closed door. "Did

something happen to my ball?" When Aurora had gone out to the basketball court earlier, he had warned her not to let anything happen to his brand-new, regulation NBA ball.

Aurora's door flew open. "Those idiots!" she cried. "They teased Rosa Linda and me. They took the ball away from us. They're the biggest jerks! I wanna get outta here! I hate this place!"

"Who took the ball away?" asked Hector.

"Those *pendejos!* The Discípulos! They think they own the place! They just come and kick everyone out!"

"My new ball?"

"It wasn't my fault!"

"You have to get out of the playground the minute you see them coming!"

"I didn't see them, all right? Rosa Linda and I were playing Pig, and they just showed up."

"Damn it! That was my brand-new ball!" Hector spun around angrily and headed back to the kitchen table.

"I'll buy you a new one, all right?" Aurora yelled after him.

When Hector walked by the sofa, Filiberto said quietly, "What you gonna do about it?" The cheetah had latched on to the gazelle's neck.

"What am I supposed to do?" said Hector, irritated.

"You want me to go out there and get killed? They can have the *pinche bola!*"

Filiberto shook his head. He was only twenty years old, but he pushed himself up from the sofa like a sixty-year-old man. He slipped his arms and head into a white T-shirt.

"What are you doing?" Hector asked.

Aurora came out of her room just as the screen door closed.

"Where's he going?" She sounded worried.

"He's crazy," said Hector. He moved to the front window and opened the curtains just enough to peer out.

Aurora yelled through the screen, "Filiberto!"

He stopped and turned around.

Aurora said, "Filiberto, listen to me—if you go over there, you'll piss them off."

He responded in a kind, almost elderly voice. "Don't worry, Mayita. I'll be right back."

He had taken only a few barefoot steps when Aurora bolted after him. "I'm going with you," she said.

Aurora and Filiberto walked side by side toward the basketball court. Hector hesitated until they were halfway there, then tentatively followed.

Filiberto stopped at the edge of the court. His head followed the ball as it moved around, then it turned and fixed itself on a group of cars parked nearby. Hector realized immediately what he was looking at: Gloria. She was reclining on the hood of a light blue Thunderbird convertible with two other girls. Her black pants hugged her tight around the hips and calves; it looked as if she was posing for a car magazine.

Hector could swear she perked up at Filiberto's gaze. Filiberto stared at Gloria, and everyone else stared at Filiberto. One by one the Discípulos stopped playing and stood frozen on the court. The ball dropped from Joey's hands and rolled to Filiberto's feet. Only when Filiberto stooped to pick it up did his eyes move away from Gloria. Filiberto handed the basketball to Aurora and gently pushed her behind him. Then he scanned the crowd of stunned Discípulos and with outstretched hands asked if anyone wanted anything from him.

Joey took a few steps toward him. "What you looking at, *ése?*" he asked Filiberto menacingly.

Everyone seemed tense except Filiberto. "What am I looking at?" Filiberto rested his eyes on Gloria once again. "I'm looking at heaven."

Hector wanted to turn around and head back home. A feeling of dread invaded him.

Joey stood there dazed, as if physically struck by Filiberto's words. Then he stuttered, "*Pendejo,* that's Chava's *ruca, ése.*"

Aurora tugged at Filiberto's arm. Finally, after looking fearlessly in Gloria's direction once more, he let Aurora pull him away.

"You just made a big mistake, *puto*. A big mistake. No one does that to Chava's *ruca, ése.*" Joey spit at Filiberto's back, but it missed him by a long shot.

Hector turned toward home and walked slowly enough for Filiberto and Aurora to catch up. Filiberto brushed right by Hector, tossing the basketball to him with a smirk of derision. Hector could feel Joey and the other Discípulos still watching them.

"That was pretty stupid," Hector hissed at him. "Why'd you do that?"

Filiberto turned to glare at Hector. *Why* didn't *you do that?* he seemed to be asking.

Then Aurora spoke. "Do you know that girl?"

"Mmm," said Filiberto.

"Chava is the *head* of the Discípulos," Aurora said.

"I know."

"Oh, man," moaned Hector. He had spent his life evading the Discípulos, and now, in a flash, he was on their radar.

Aurora asked Filiberto, "Do you think she's actually pretty or just slut-pretty?"

"Pretty," Fili answered immediately.

"I think to be actually pretty you also have to be smart."

"Maybe she's smart, too."

"I can't see how, if she's hanging out with the Discípulos."

After a few more steps, Aurora asked, "Why do you do that, anyway?"

"What?"

"Look for trouble like that?"

Because he doesn't give a shit about anybody else, Hector said to himself.

"I just do things. I don't worry about it. Is that looking for trouble?"

"Duh, yeah," Hector said. For a moment he thought Filiberto might turn around and smack him. Aurora laughed. But Filiberto was serious. "I don't know why I do things. Sometimes I can't help it."

"That's what Papá said about drinking and smoking," said Aurora.

Fili just shrugged.

"You're going to see her, aren't you?" she asked.

"Man, you do and we're all dead," Hector blurted out.

"I won't make the first move," Filiberto said to Aurora, ignoring him.

"And if she comes after you?" she asked.

"Then it's something that's supposed to happen . . . *qué no?* How can I say no to that?"

"Come on, man," Hector said, feeling himself grow more and more agitated. "Do you know what you're saying?"

"Promise you won't make the first move," said Aurora.

"Te lo prometo."

"You can't make *any* move! First, second, or anything! Don't you know who you're dealing with? You're going to screw all of us!" Hector stomped ahead of them.

Behind him he heard Aurora say, "Don't bullshit me, Fili." She was stern, like a little mother. "You better keep your promise."

2

The next morning Hector's reading was interrupted by a knock at the screen door. He froze when he saw her standing there.

"Hey," she said.

"Hey."

"I'm Gloria."

He knew who she was. Before yesterday at the basketball court, he had seen her riding in Chava's white Impala, snuggling close to him. Hector looked over her shoulder to see if there was anyone on the street behind her.

"It's just me," she said with a nervous giggle.

"What is it?" He didn't mean to sound as rude as he did.

"You must be his brother," she said.

"Whose?"

"Filiberto."

"Yeah. Uh-huh."

"He wouldn't be in now, would he?"

"I don't know." Stupid as it sounded, it was true. Hector had jumped out of bed that morning without noticing whether Filiberto was in, even though they shared the same room.

"I just need to talk to him for a few minutes, if he's in."

"Uh, let me check." He felt dazed by her, and scared. Without inviting her inside, he headed down the hall slowly, trying to buy enough time to recover his senses. He opened the bedroom door to see that Filiberto's bed had not been slept in. Once again he had stayed out all night. When Hector returned, Gloria was staring at her feet.

"He's not in. He must have left with my sister and my mother, to go shopping, in Juárez, you know?"

She looked disappointed.

"Sorry," he said.

"It's okay." She waved good-bye.

"You want to leave a message?" he offered suddenly. He didn't know why.

She turned around, hesitated. For a second it seemed as if she had decided to leave well enough alone. But then she said, "Okay. Do you have something to write with?"

Hector tore a piece of paper from one of his notebooks on the kitchen table and grabbed a pencil. He opened the screen door just enough to hand her the paper and pencil. If anyone ever asked him, he could say he never let her in. *She* came to see *them*. He had to open the door to see who it was, but he never let her in.

Gloria sat down on the small step in front of the apartment and started scrawling on the loose-leaf paper. Hector decided to go inside and act as if he had a thousand things to do. When he came out again, she was gone. Tucked in the mailbox was the paper, folded into a tiny square. He took it inside and locked the door behind him. He read the message. *Filiberto: Call me. 555-7560. Gloria.*

Hector considered tearing it into tiny pieces and flushing the confetti down the toilet. She was Chava's woman. How could she think she could just come over and drag his whole family into the stinking world of the Discípulos? They had worked too hard to stay out of trouble's way.

But he changed his mind about destroying the note. It

was proof that *she* had made the first move, not Fili. He took out the Band-Aid tin he kept things in and stuck the paper in there. Then he put it back in his desk drawer, where Filiberto would never see it.

Filiberto didn't tell anyone that they would have a guest for the Sunday meal. He woke up when Conchita, Hector, and Aurora returned from ten o'clock Mass. He plopped onto the sofa next to Hector as Conchita, in the kitchen, filled the air with the smell of her *mole* sauce.

Filiberto rubbed his eyes. "How was Mass?"

"Same as always." The subject of going to church, or more precisely, of his never going, was a hot topic between Conchita and Filiberto, and Hector didn't want to get in the middle of it.

"That's good."

Hector didn't move his eyes from the magazine he was reading. It seemed as if Filiberto was trying to engage him in some kind of small talk, to get in his good graces.

"How's school going?"

"Fine."

"Still getting good grades?"

Filiberto already knew the answer to that one. Only last week Conchita had proudly shown him Hector's name on the sophomore honor roll. Filiberto hadn't cared at the time, and Hector knew he didn't now either.

"Yeah," Hector said warily, like someone who knows he is about to be hit up for a loan.

"That's good, man." He lifted his head, tilted it toward the kitchen, and sniffed. "That smell always makes me think of him," said Filiberto.

Hector nodded. This was about the time Papá would always put on one of his Cuco Sánchez records. Aurora called the Sunday noontime meal "Mexican Hour" because during that time Filemón usually got carried away with nostalgia. It was also a meal Filiberto never missed. He could disappear for days at a time, but somehow he was always there for Sunday *mole*.

"How long has it been?"

Hector had a fleeting, hateful thought about how Filiberto, who was so close to Papá, didn't even remember the date of his death. He tried to knock that thought out of his mind before it stirred up the familiar resentment toward Filiberto for leaving him to deal with all the details of the funeral.

"It's been thirteen months," Hector answered. He raised the magazine to his face before Filiberto could read his thoughts: *I will never forgive you for disappearing at a time like that.*

Hector's thoughts were interrupted by a familiar voice.

"Hey!" It was Gloria. She was at the screen door.

Filiberto sprang up from the sofa to let her in. Now Hector understood why he had been acting so strangely.

"Hey," he said to her in a way that was warm and grateful. "You eaten yet?"

"Not yet," she said shyly.

Hector's heart beat hard against his chest. All he could think about was the note hidden in the Band-Aid tin. Had Fili found it?

Conchita came out of the kitchen, wiping her hands on her red apron. "Mamá, this is Gloria. She came over for some of your *mole*," said Filiberto.

Conchita gave Gloria a good looking over. It was the first time Filiberto had ever introduced a girlfriend to her. In the brief second it took her to grasp Gloria's hand, Hector saw his mother take in all available information about the girl.

He read Conchita's rapid judgment. This was not the kind of girl who would turn Filiberto into the kind of man she wished him to be.

"*Mucho gusto,*" said Conchita, testing to see if the girl knew Spanish.

"Hi," responded Gloria.

Hector could no longer hide behind his magazine. He shook Gloria's hand quickly and was relieved when she acted as if she were meeting him for the first time, too.

"*Bueno,*" said Conchita, "welcome to our home. Hector, come help me make the lemonade."

"Who is she?" Conchita asked when they were alone in the kitchen.

"La Gloria," answered Hector.

"What's the matter, why do you look so angry?"

"That girl is nothing but trouble, and now he brings her here."

"Why is she trouble? Tell me."

"Because she's . . . she's a—" He stopped himself from saying a word that would have shocked his mother. "She's a girl who goes out with the Discípulos."

"The Discípulos? Oh." Conchita was more confused than upset. "How does Filiberto know her? It must be all right, if he invited her."

Hector shot her an exasperated look. She had no idea

what Filiberto was getting them into. "I'm going to my room," he said.

"Hector, wait." Conchita grabbed him by the arm. "You're going to eat with us. Don't be disrespectful to your brother's guest."

Hector shook her off and stomped out of the kitchen. On his way to his room, he passed the sofa where Filiberto and Gloria were talking softly. He could feel Gloria turn her head toward him, but he didn't look in her direction.

About half an hour later Conchita called everyone to the table. Hector and Aurora emerged from their rooms. Aurora stopped in her tracks when she saw Gloria.

"What's she doing here?" she blurted out.

"Aurora!" Conchita shot her a look that said, *Be quiet, behave, sit down, and be a lady.* Conchita looked at the food in front of her, crossed herself in thanks, and then tried to start up a friendly conversation.

"So," said Conchita, "where did you two meet?"

"Yeah, Fili. Where *did* you meet?" Aurora asked accusingly.

Filiberto smiled at Aurora. Gloria blushed. Hector scooped up his food as if someone had put a gun to his head and told him he had to eat it all in less than three minutes.

"At the garage where Fili works. I took my mom's car

to get the brakes fixed." Gloria looked at Filiberto for confirmation. She opened her mouth to say more, but just then Hector started coughing and turning red. Aurora reached over and whacked him between his shoulders. Hector lifted his hands to say he was okay.

"So," Conchita continued, once the coughing fit was over, "you go to Ysleta High?"

"Right now I'm going to school to study hair design and working at a beauty shop."

Aurora looked at Hector and rolled her eyes as if to say: *Hair design? Pleeeaaase!* Hector bit his tongue so as not to laugh. He kicked Aurora's leg under the table.

"Ay!" yelled Aurora.

Gloria giggled, for no apparent reason. Filiberto gave Hector a menacing look.

"But you finished high school, right?" Conchita was relentless.

"Well, actually, I had to leave at the end of my junior year. My father was out on workers' comp, and my mother doesn't work, and I have two younger sisters and one baby brother."

"Ahh," sighed Conchita.

Just when it looked as if Conchita was ready to give up the questioning, Aurora asked Gloria point-blank: "What happened to Chava?"

Hector gulped a piece of unchewed chicken and almost choked again.

"Aurora," said Filiberto, more pleading than commanding.

"Who's Chava?" asked Conchita, bewildered.

"He's only the head of the Discípulos," said Aurora, shooting an angry glance at Filiberto. *Serves you right for breaking your promise,* it said.

Hector stopped eating, his fork and knife frozen in the act of cutting. He couldn't help but enjoy watching Filiberto and Gloria squirm.

"Aurora," said Filiberto without raising his voice, "Gloria's my guest."

"That's okay," said Gloria. Hector noticed that she had hardly touched her food. He almost, but not quite, felt sorry for her. Gloria turned toward Conchita. "Chava's the guy I was going out with. I broke up with him."

"Oh," said Conchita. She didn't know what else to say. Everyone started pushing food around their plates as a silence thick as concrete filled the room. Only Filiberto continued eating.

Hector felt something rise in his esophagus. At first he thought that he was about to vomit the *mole* and rice he had just finished shoveling in. But what came out of his mouth were words, bitter and dripping with anger.

"What's he going to do now?"

"What?" Gloria sputtered.

Filiberto put his hands on the table and stared coldly at Hector. Even Aurora looked scared of where the conversation was going.

"I mean, is he going to come after us? What's your *vato* going to do now, kill us all?" Hector's hands, still clutching a fork and knife, trembled, and his face darkened with blood.

"Hector, *contrólate*," pleaded Conchita.

"Breathe!" Aurora ordered.

Filiberto glared at him, and Hector glared right back. At that moment he felt that he could take on Filiberto. He was the taller of the two. Maybe he was stronger, too. If Filiberto wanted to go at it, he was ready. Hector shouted, "Well? What do you think he's going to do? You think he's just going to let her go? Use your *cabeza* instead of your *bolas* for once in your life, man!"

Filiberto stood up, his eyes shimmering. Hector had seen that expression in his eyes many times before and on a few occasions had felt the blows that followed.

"Go ahead and hit me!" yelled Hector. "That's what you do best, isn't it? You know how gangs work! You do something to them, and they do something back to you. You know I'm right!"

Gloria looked ready to cry, but Hector knew she recognized the truth in his words. Aurora left the table and went over to Filiberto. She hugged him, pinning his arms like a human straitjacket.

"No, no, no!" she repeated.

"Hector, go to your room right now," ordered Conchita, but her voice was weak and lacked authority.

Without a word, Filiberto disentangled himself from Aurora's arms and stretched his hand out to Gloria. She grabbed it and stood up. As Hector went to his room, he looked back to see Fili leading her out of the house as coolly as a couple on the way to the dance floor.

4

At school the following morning, Sammy told Hector and Rosa Linda told Aurora that Filiberto was in deep shit. The story Sammy told was slightly different from the one Rosa Linda told. But Sammy's brother Ramiro was a Discípulo, so Hector decided that Sammy's story was more trustworthy.

According to Sammy, Filiberto and Gloria went over to the Discípulos' hangout on Sunday afternoon and asked to speak to Chava. Sammy recounted the whole story: "Chava was already pissed, because Gloria had tried to break up with him the night before. He told her *que no, que* no one breaks up with him. She tried to argue with him, but he just got more and more pissed until he finally told her he didn't want to hear any more bullshit and he walked out. I guess she didn't tell him why she wanted to break up with him.

"That was Saturday night. Then, on Sunday afternoon, Chava's hanging with the *vatos,* just shooting some pool or whatever, when in comes Filiberto and Gloria. Man, that just isn't done, *ése.* Least your *carnal* shoulda done is try to set up a meeting in private when none of the Discípulos are around. What was Chava supposed to do? He's gonna let someone show disrespect in front of his people? So they just show up, the two of them, and ask to speak to him in private. Man, your *pinche* brother couldn't have picked a worse time. The Discípulos are trying to join up with La Raza, this other gang with ties to the Texas Mexicans who have ties to the Mejicanos out of L.A. So here's Chava trying to make it into the big time, and people are looking at him, seeing if he's got the balls to play with the big guys, and then someone comes and takes his *ruca* from him. Shit, man, the whole timing couldn't be worse. Anyway, La Gloria's begging Chava to understand, and even your brother, man, he's practically humiliating himself, saying he doesn't want any trouble, he's coming in peace, one *carnal* to another, to see if they can work things out. Shit! What's Chava supposed to do, man? It looks bad, real bad to lose your *ruca* like that.

Pinche Gloria, what she shoulda done is ask Chava in private to just say that he's tired of her—then, after a while, she could hook up with your *carnal, ése.* Since when is your brother Mr. Civilized, anyway? Shit! So Ramiro says that the only reason Chava doesn't finish your brother right then and there is 'cause number one, there's a whole bunch of people playing billiards in the front room, you know, over at Carolina's. And number two, Chava's got to talk to the Council before, you know, he gets into it with other *raza.* That's like a rule. No shit, man, Chava's got to take the thing up with them. Man, you gotta get a hold of your *carnal, ése.* I don't know what the Council's gonna say, but whatever it is, it ain't gonna be good for him."

Aurora heard a similar story from Rosa Linda, who had heard it from Denise, who had heard it directly from Gloria's best friend, Nieves. "Gloria called Nieves from some motel on Alameda," Rosa Linda said. "She and Filiberto got a room there—sorry, but it's true—and while Filiberto was out getting some beer, Gloria told Nieves to go home and get some of her things. I guess Gloria's mom is used to La Gloria spending the night out, which tells you a lot right there. She told Nieves that she and Filiberto had tried to talk to Chava that afternoon, but Chava was being very stubborn. Nieves asked her what she was going to do, and Gloria said she didn't know. 'Why don't you run away with

Filiberto?' Nieves asked her. And get this, Gloria told her she wasn't sure she wanted to run away with Filiberto. Gloria's all confused again. She likes both of them, the big *puta* that she is. You know, before Chava she went out with a cowboy gringo who lives near her, and there's been others. She thinks she's the Queen of Sheba, but she's just dirt. Just 'cause her mother's a *gabacha,* she thinks she's Miss Universe. Anyways, Gloria told Nieves that she's afraid for her life because there's no telling what Chava'll do. She wanted Nieves to get in touch with Chava and tell him that she needs to talk to him alone. She was having second thoughts about whether she did the right thing with Filiberto. Get this, Gloria wants Nieves to hint to Chava that Gloria's maybe ready to ask him to take her back—she wants Nieves to see how he'd react to that. Meantime she's in Fuck City Motel with your brother. *Qué bicha!*"

5

On Tuesday afternoon, Aurora came home later than usual.
Conchita was out with the ladies of the Altar Guild, deco-
rating the church. Hector was lying in his bed, thinking
about what his brother had done, when he heard Aurora
enter. He sprang out of bed and almost jumped on her.

"Where the hell have you been? It's nearly five-thirty!"

"Settle down. I had to go someplace after school." She
struggled out of a knapsack that hung heavy on her back.

Hector was too impatient to ask again where she'd been.
"We're in deep shit with the Discípulos," he declared.

"I know," said Aurora.

"I knew something bad was going to happen. I just knew it."

"Okay, you were right."

"I wish people would listen to me around here."

"Yeah. Yeah."

"Shit! We spend all our lives keeping our heads low, and now he goes and does this!"

"I got the picture, all right? We have to figure out what we're going to do."

"It's his problem."

"Hector, come on, he's our brother. Besides, it's all our problem."

"There's nothing we can do."

"I did something." There was a tinge of pride in her voice.

"What?"

"I went to ask for help."

"When? Who?"

"Today, after school. I went to the police."

"The police? Are you nuts?"

"Well, we had to do something. Otherwise Chava's going to go after Filiberto."

"And you think talking to the police will help? What do you think Chava'll do when he finds out?"

"The police can help. They can warn the guy. Tell him

they know what he's thinking of doing and he better not do it."

"Just tell me what you did."

"I went to the police department and talked to this lady."

"A policewoman?"

"Yeah. No, she was a social worker. She deals with gangs and stuff."

"What'd you tell her?"

"Everything. When I got there, this big policewoman at the front desk asked me a whole bunch of questions. Then she made me wait for about an hour."

"Okay, okay. What happened then?"

"Finally this woman named Rosario Garza walks out and asks me to follow her."

"What exactly did you tell her?"

"I started at the beginning, with how Filiberto went to get your basketball, and then I told her about him and Gloria—what Rosa Linda said. I told her we were in danger—all of us, but mostly Filiberto. She knew all about the Discípulos, and all the other gangs. They keep track of them. She was pretty good."

Hector couldn't stop pacing. "Yeah, yeah, but I mean, why the hell didn't you tell me you were going to talk to the police?"

"Hector, listen to me. You would have said no, right? Nobody in this family ever does anything. Everyone just sits there praying or drinking, like there's nothing that can be done."

"That's not fair."

"I did the right thing. Mrs. Garza's going to help."

"How? By talking to Chava?"

"She can find another place for us to live. That's what social workers do. She told me."

"What? We're not going to move from here. This is where we live."

"You like it here? Fine. Stay, then."

"Look, it's not that easy. This is our home. This is where Papá wanted us to be."

"Mamá, not Papá."

"What does that mean?"

"She's the one who wanted us to be here. He hated it here."

"He did not."

"Hector, why do you protect her so much?"

"I don't. I don't protect her."

"Okay, you don't."

"What's the matter with you, anyway? What's gotten into you?"

"Nothing."

"Look. Just tell me once and for all how you left things with this Mrs. Rosario."

"Mrs. Garza. Her first name is Rosario. She just listened, okay? She's going to look into it. Don't worry. She said she would work behind the scenes. There isn't much she can do about Gloria and Filiberto going out, though. I mean, what can she do?"

"Exactly."

"She did say talking to Chava was a possibility. Like telling him that if anything happens to our family, they'll haul his ass to jail no matter what."

"Oh, great! That's just what we need."

"She just mentioned it as a possibility. She won't do it until she talks to Mamá. She wants to come over."

"When?"

"I don't know; soon. She was going to look into some things first, talk to some people, think of some options. She listened to me. She took me seriously. She's interested, all right?"

"You may have just screwed all of us real good."

"I told her about you."

"What about me? What do you mean?"

"I told her you made the honor roll. How you want to go to college. I told her I want to be a nurse. I told her all of that."

"You're a piece of work. Seriously, Aurora, you really are."

"Is that so bad? Huh? Is it so bad to ask for help?"

"We don't need any help. It's a helpless situation. And it's none of your damn business what I do or want to do. Stay out of it!"

"Hector!"

"Who appointed you queen bee? Who the hell made you head of this family?"

"Okay. Hector, breathe. I did it. Get over it."

6

The first thing Hector noticed when he walked over to Gloria's house the following afternoon was the giant pecan tree in front. Its shade created a dark patch in the middle of the road, where two little girls played with naked Barbies. One Barbie was being wedged into the passenger seat of a toy Mustang convertible; the other one lay, legs crossed, on the hood.

"Is Gloria home?" he asked when they finally looked up at him.

"Gloriaaaa!" yelled the girl who was cramming the Barbie into the pink plastic car. The other girl put one finger in her mouth and looked down when Hector smiled at her.

"Gloriaaaa!" she yelled again, making Hector wince. The shy girl put her fingers in her ears and closed her eyes.

"*Quééé?*" someone from inside the house yelled back angrily.

Hector assumed it was Gloria's mother who appeared at the door. She held a diaperless baby in her arms and seemed annoyed that someone was in her front yard.

Hector walked up to the door so he wouldn't have to shout. "Is Gloria in?"

Without a word, the woman turned around and disappeared inside. "Make it quick," he heard her say to someone.

"Hey, Hector! What are you doing here?" It was Gloria. She was buttoning up her blouse.

"Hey," he responded.

"Is everything okay?" She had buttoned as much as she was going to button.

"Oh, yeah."

"Wanna come in?" Hector could tell she didn't really want him to.

"No, no thanks."

She stepped outside. The shy girl ran over to grab one of

Gloria's legs. She started sucking her thumb. Gloria rubbed her head and said, "Say hi to Hector."

The little girl shook her head. Gloria walked Hector toward the pecan tree with the girl still hanging on to her leg.

"What's going on?" she asked him.

"Actually, I came to apologize."

"Why?" She picked up the little girl, who buried her head in Gloria's shoulder.

"About the other day. At our house."

"Oh, don't worry. I wasn't offended."

"I . . . we . . . we didn't treat you right."

"Hey, you were worried."

From one of the windows behind them came a shout: "Gloriaa! The dishes."

"I'm coming!" Gloria shouted back.

"I should go. I just wanted to stop by. To apologize."

"Oh, you're sweet." The little girl wiggled in Gloria's arms, and Gloria put her down. "Wait, wait." She took a tissue out of her jeans and wiped green stuff from the girl's nose. "Yucch." The girl ran back to her toys.

"Your sisters?" *What a stupid question,* he thought at once.

"And a baby brother inside." She said it as if she couldn't believe it herself.

"Are you the oldest?"

"Yup."

"Wow." Hector was having trouble thinking of things to say. After all the time he had spent debating about whether he should come see her, he had ended up doing it at the last second. It was a mistake. All the things he did like that, last-second, get-it-over-with kinds of things, turned out to be mistakes.

"Come on, I'll walk a little with you," she said. She pulled him gently toward the road. The walk to her house in the heat must have affected him, because he felt his legs go wobbly.

"You okay?" she asked with a smile. She seemed to be aware of what her touch could do.

"Yeah," he said.

She let go of his arm and stuck her hands in the pockets of her cutoffs. "You didn't really come here to apologize, did you?"

"Yes, I did."

They stopped. They could see a red truck coming toward them on the dirt road. Gloria turned around and yelled at her two little sisters, *"Carro!"* The two girls pushed their pink Mustang out of the road and into the cotton fields. Gloria and Hector waited for the truck to go by. The driver was a young man in a white cowboy hat. He slowed down to leer at Gloria. Gloria grabbed Hector's arm again. Then the driver accelerated, kicking gravel and dust in their faces.

"*Pendejo,*" said Gloria.

"Who's he?"

"Some guy who thinks he's hot because he has a red truck. Asshole."

Gloria's mother was at the door. "Gloria, I'm not bull-shitting about the dishes."

"I'll be right there, Mother," Gloria said calmly, one grown-up to another. Then she grabbed Hector's hand and pulled him out of the cotton field. "Look at your shoes."

They were covered in mud—he had stepped on the recently irrigated field. He also had a ball of cotton stuck to the front of his shirt. She peeled it off. "You're right," he said to her.

"About what?"

"About why I came here."

"Tell me."

"You see . . . Filiberto . . . He . . . he does things some-times."

"Yeah?"

"I'm not here to talk behind his back. It's just that for a

long time, for a long time now, we've been making it okay. We've been basically making it, even after my father died. We never had any trouble with anyone. We've kept our heads low."

"So . . ."

"So . . ."

"So you think I'm trouble." She didn't sound mad or anything.

"Not you. It's just that, maybe it's not worth it. You and Filiberto, maybe it's not worth it for anyone. I mean, is it? I mean, it's not like Chava's going to let you be. And Filiberto . . ."

"What about him?"

"Filiberto. He . . ."

"Say it."

"He's had many girlfriends. I've seen him. He's not the type that settles down."

Gloria laughed. She searched in her pocket for something, then pulled out a stick of gum in a turquoise wrapper. She tore it in half and offered him a piece. "Want some?"

"No thanks."

She stuck both pieces in her mouth. "Filiberto's different. He's the only person I know who doesn't really care whether I leave him or not. Every other guy I've known has always been afraid of losing me. They worry about it all the time. That guy in the red truck, I stopped going out with him when I met Chava, and he's still afraid of losing me. He's a big jerk. A bigger jerk than Chava ever was. I thought that because he was Anglo, maybe he'd be different. He was worse. At least Chava respects me, in his own way, believe it or not."

Hector started to talk, but she interrupted. "I know about Filiberto's girlfriends and how he doesn't stay with them for very long. Don't you think I know? Maybe that's why I like him."

Hector knew right then that nothing good was going to come out of this visit. He felt a penetrating, pulsating pain above his right eyebrow.

"Listen." She started walking again. "I'm going to talk to Chava again, alone this time. It'll be okay—after a while, I mean. Don't get me wrong, it's not going to be that easy. The Discípulos don't like Filiberto. How can they like someone who's not afraid of them? But they'll listen to Chava. He'll understand eventually. I know him better than anybody else. Believe me."

Hector wanted to believe her, but he found her words almost incomprehensible. How could a person like Chava, someone who got into fights and dealt drugs, love and respect a woman? And why, if he loved her, would he ever let her go? Hector wanted to believe that could happen, and all this could go away, but he felt like he was missing the necessary education in love and relationships. Maybe he had to live more, live harder, like Filiberto, to understand these things.

They reached the end of the dirt road. "Don't worry," she said.

"I'm not," he lied. He was more worried than ever. Hector now realized that the situation was more complicated, more difficult, and more dangerous than he had imagined.

"Hey," she said.

He turned around.

"He talks about you all the time. He says you're the smart one. He's real proud of you."

"Who?"

"Fili."

"I'll see you," he said, walking off before she could see his blush. Despite his misgivings about the mess they were in, on his way home he considered the possibility that Gloria was a better person than he had thought.

7

Hector had just started reading a book called the *Bhagavad-Gita* when Filiberto walked into their room on Friday night. Fili hadn't been home since the Sunday meal with Gloria. They knew he was all right, because Conchita had called his boss at Manny's Automotive to make sure he'd been showing up for work.

Filiberto looked as if he hadn't shaved in a few days, and he was wearing the same blue jeans and white T-shirt he'd had on the previous Sunday, when all hell had broken loose.

Hector took out a ruler in case he needed to underline a

passage. Filiberto sat down on the edge of his own bed, and Hector saw peripherally that he was holding his head in his two hands. It made Hector want to apologize for the way he had behaved and for going to talk to Gloria, but part of him still believed he had said and done the right things. He was sorry he had made Gloria uncomfortable, but Filiberto had been even more reckless than usual lately. He decided not to speak until Filiberto did. He didn't have to wait long.

"Let's go out and get something to drink," said Filiberto. He sounded tired.

"What, right now?" Hector looked at the windup alarm clock ticking on his desk. It was 10:30.

"Yeah, why not? We need to talk."

Hector wondered why they couldn't talk right there, but something about Filiberto's manner made him close the book and get up. They were careful not to wake Conchita and Aurora as they left the house.

They drove in silence toward Juárez. As usual, Hector was apprehensive about his brother. Filiberto was unpredictable, always on the edge of trouble. One moment he was serene, and the next he looked as if he would kill you in a blink.

Hector remembered too many things to feel comfortable around Filiberto. There were too many wrestling matches when all of a sudden the horsing around turned serious, and Hector found himself in a choking head clinch. There was the time when Hector had lightly slapped Aurora on the back of the head after one of her typical smart-ass remarks. Filiberto came out of nowhere and, with one shove to the chest, landed Hector on his butt. "Don't ever hit a girl," was all Filiberto had said.

Now Hector was full of foreboding. He could feel it in his bones. Filiberto was going to hurt him before the night was over.

They stopped at a place with a white-and-red neon sign that flashed EL CORRALITO. When they entered, everyone in the place greeted Filiberto. He headed toward a table near a multicolored jukebox. A pretty girl with Mexican features came over to take their order.

"Sandra," Filiberto said, pointing, "this is my brother, Hector." The girl shook Hector's hand with a firm and warm grip.

"*Mucho gusto,* Hector."

"'Pleased to meet you, Hector,'" Filiberto said to Sandra in a teacherly tone. "Sandra is learning English," he explained unnecessarily to Hector.

"My English not very good. I am happy to meet you. I heard many things about you." She spoke slowly, as if reading the words from a distance.

Hector looked away from her, embarrassed. "Thank

you," he said. What could Fili have told her? Was she just parroting an English phrase she once heard?

"*Lo mismo de siempre?* Two Carta Blancas?" she asked.

"*Una Tecate para él,*" Filiberto responded without asking Hector.

Sandra brought two beers. Filiberto took a sip, lit a cigarette, then cleared his throat. It seemed to Hector that Filiberto needed the drink and smoke in order to speak. Hector raised the bottle quickly to his lips and took a giant gulp. He started coughing.

"Go slow," said Filiberto.

He's teaching me like Papá taught him, thought Hector. He shoved the beer aside.

Then Hector broke the silence. "I shouldn't have said what I said the other day, when you brought Gloria."

"You said what you wanted to say."

"I didn't have to say it in front of her."

"Listen, *carnalito.*" Was it the first time Filiberto had ever called him little brother? "You don't have to apologize. If anything, it's me who should apologize. I really went and messed things up."

The words were so uncharacteristic of Filiberto that Hector didn't know how to respond.

"I've messed up in many ways." Filiberto turned around to check the clock in back of the bar. He seemed impatient to get to a certain point in the conversation. "I want to talk to you about something." He shifted uncomfortably in his seat. "You've done a good job with your studies."

What does that have to do with anything? wondered Hector.

"You need to keep on doing that no matter what."

Hector felt his stomach sink. "You say that like something's going to happen . . ."

"It's just that I'm in this thing now. The Discípulos are . . . Even I don't understand how they think. They have all these rules, this world they've created."

"Do you know something? Did they say something to you?" Hector leaned forward. "I mean, I know about the Discípulos and the meeting the Council was going to have about you. Sammy told me." He started to say something about going to see Gloria, then decided to wait until Fili brought it up.

"I tried talking to them. 'Don't do anything stupid, Filiberto,' I said to myself. 'What would Hector do?'" Filiberto gave out a short laugh. "I went up to talk to this *vato*, Chava. 'I fell in love with this girl, and she fell in love with me,' I tried to tell him. 'It's not that hard to understand. It happens all the time. People don't have to kill each other about it, right?' You would've been proud of me, *carnal*. I didn't lose it."

Hector felt so many conflicting emotions. Fili wanted to make *him* proud? But he didn't allow himself to dwell on that thought. "So, did you hear? About the Council, I mean. What they decided?"

Filiberto shrugged. Hector couldn't tell whether the shrug meant that Filiberto hadn't heard or that what he heard wasn't worth talking about.

Fili continued. "Gloria tried talking to the guy, too. Before she came over to the house on Sunday. He doesn't want to hear us out." He stopped and stared into space for a minute.

Hector's throat was dry, but he didn't want the rest of his warm beer. "Can I get something else?" He lifted his bottle toward Filiberto. "Maybe some water?"

Filiberto barked another laugh and signaled to Sandra, who seemed to be watching them. She took their order of a beer and a Coke, and as they waited for her to return, they sat in silence—an easy one this time. It was strange for Hector to feel at ease, given what they were talking about. Still, Hector looked down at the table, afraid to see what was in his brother's eyes. Was this where Fili disappeared almost every night? Did drinking give him courage? It hadn't seemed to do that for Papá.

Hector summoned his own courage. "Filiberto." He took a deep breath. "Are you sure Gloria loves you?"

"The thing is, people are just people. Gloria's been around. So have I. See these women here?" He nodded toward a table where three women sat. "They're just people. Sometimes they tell the truth, sometimes they lie. That one who just winked at you, she's pretty, isn't she? You can pay to sleep with her, but she'll never let you kiss her. She only kisses the one person in the world she loves."

"But . . ."

Filiberto kept on. "Gloria thinks I can offer her something better than Chava, but that's scary to her. It's like she can't break the chains that tie her to Chava. We're all slaves, Hector, to something or other." He raised his beer bottle and briefly held it in front of him before taking another sip. "Am I sure she loves me? In her own way she does."

"I didn't mean to say that she isn't right for you."

"You did. But that's okay. You're just human, and you're a slave, too, even if you don't know it. But what I wanted to tell you, *carnalito,* is that I think you're one of the few who can be free. You have to make sure you make it, *carnal. Me entiendes?*"

"Sort of."

"Filemón, Mamá, Aurora, we all put our hopes on you. You're the one. Ever since you were this little, and we saw how you liked to read more than anything else. That's why Filemón went to those night classes to learn English. He

133

wanted to speak to you in English. He didn't want anything holding you back."

Hector felt dizzy and wondered whether his one swallow of beer could have affected him. Maybe it was all the cigarette smoke. Filiberto turned around to look at the clock again.

"I have to leave you here for a while. I've got to meet Chava. That's what this Council that decides who lives and dies decided. We need to work things out."

"Where are you going? What did they say?"

Fili ignored Hector's questions. "I want to give you something." He reached into his back pocket and pulled out a little green book. "This is a savings account Filemón started when you were about three years old. He had twenty-five dollars of his pay deposited into it every week. Before he died, he set it up so that either you or I can take money out. I got a form you're supposed to sign—after that you can make withdrawals. Hold on, let me get a witness. Pepe!" Filiberto called to the man behind the bar. *"Ven!"*

Filiberto grabbed the pen from Pepe's shirt pocket and gave it to Hector. Still feeling woozy, Hector signed, then Pepe signed. *"Gracias,"* Filiberto said to Pepe with a nod.

"Why are we doing this now?" Hector asked, though he knew the answer. He stood up on shaky legs. "I don't want to stay here. Let me come with you." His voice was shrill, like a whiny toddler.

"I'm just going to meet Chava. We're going to work it out. I need to let the *vato* save face in front of his people. *Por qué no?* I have a plan, *carnalito*."

Don't go, Hector thought, *you'll get killed.* The room started spinning, and he sank back down into his chair.

"Listen to me. The money is for you to go to college. Filemón didn't want me to use it for anything else. I didn't even use it for his funeral." Filiberto paused, and Hector knew that in his clumsy way he was apologizing for abandoning the family then.

"I'm going to do this thing. Then you'll do your thing. You'll be a free man." Filiberto stood up abruptly, turned his head away from Hector, and said in a voice loud enough to be heard across the room, "I have to go now. Talk to Sandra, she's a nice girl."

As he left, Hector thought, *I'm never going to see my brother again.*

8

Hector glanced at the bar's clock, in the shape of a waterfall, with flickering lights that simulated moving water. Sandra had been sitting with him off and on, but at that moment— 1:35 A.M.—she was helping Matilde waitress the crowd.

El Corralito now seemed a different place from the one he and Filiberto had entered only two hours before. Now it was lively with laughter and loud boasting and even an occasional Mexican *grito*. Sometime after midnight a traveling mariachi band had come in, trumpets blaring, and the place woke up.

Hector's earlier dizziness had disappeared. His mind was

clear, and clear, too, was the emotion he felt. The absence of his brother flapped through his empty chest like a hapless bird trapped inside a church. In his mind he saw his older brother pulling him in the rusty, red wagon. Then he saw Filiberto sitting next to his father on the back steps of their apartment. Filiberto was reading from a *National Geographic*, stumbling over the multisyllable words, sounding out the letters like a first grader. Papá was enjoying the company of his older son, attentively listening, oblivious to Filiberto's halting, shoddy reading.

Hector was restless, tense, and sick of his own company. But whenever he'd started to get up, he sat down again. This was where Filiberto had brought him and, for some reason, wanted him to be. Besides, Hector had no way of getting home.

Hector had looked around and caught Sandra's gaze. She was at the bar, waiting for Pepe to fill her tray with drinks, and he could tell that she had been looking at him just before he turned to see her. He waved at her spontaneously, childlike.

When her tray was filled, she walked by his table and said, "*Ahorita vengo.* I'll be right over."

"Don't worry," he'd said. But it was hard to keep sitting alone, waiting for who knows what.

During the twenty minutes or so that Sandra had managed to sit with him that night, their conversation had been inconsequential. How long had Sandra worked there? How did she find the time to go to school and do homework and also waitress? Did she live far from the bar? Had she always lived in Juárez? He learned that she had just turned eighteen a few weeks before, and he hoped he seemed older than sixteen to her. He had only begun to tell Sandra about himself when she was called to help out with the crowd. She was different from Gloria. Not as pretty maybe, but somehow more real. He wasn't nervous around her the way he was around Gloria. Not *as* nervous anyway. It was good that Sandra did not leave all the talking to him. He was glad that sooner or later she would join him again.

Now a couple started dancing. The man had on blue jeans, cowboy boots, and a baseball cap. The woman was one of the three who had been there when he first arrived and who had greeted Filiberto happily, as if they were old acquaintances. As he watched the woman dance with the cowboy, he looked for clues that she was a prostitute. She wasn't dancing provocatively. They could have been any couple, dancing more to enjoy the rhythm of the music than the feel of each other's body. She was dressed in a plain black dress that was not too short. The kind of dress a poor person might wear to a special occasion.

He opened the green savings-account book and scanned

the pages filled with dates and amounts. As Filiberto had said, there was a deposit every week, always the same amount: twenty-five dollars. He checked the last total. It was an incredible amount of money. He looked again at the last deposit date—it was only week ago. He traced the dates back until he came to the day his father died, more than a year earlier. The truth finally dawned on him: Filiberto had continued to deposit twenty-five dollars in the account every week.

At around 2:30 A.M., things quieted down enough for Sandra to sit with him again. She was out of breath and seemed agitated.

"Sorry," she said as she took a seat. She brought him a glass of ice water.

"Why?" he asked.

She thought for a few seconds and then said, "I wish I spend more time with you."

She reached over and touched his hand. He smiled and held her fingers in his. She didn't mind. He wanted to say something, but he was so tired there was no way he could speak coherently. He stayed quiet, closed his eyes, and let her caress his hand, wishing the moment didn't have to end.

But it did.

"Hector?"

He shut his eyes hard, as if doing so would also shut his ears.

"Filiberto tuvo un accidente." Her words confirmed what he had already felt. "Sebastián—he came by Ysleta. He saw the *ambulancias*. A truck crashed into a train. They said it was Filiberto."

Hector turned around, trying to find Sebastián even though he had never heard of or seen him before. He saw that everyone was looking at him with pity. Anger flashed at the thought that so many people could see what he was feeling.

"He's dead, isn't he?" he said too loudly.

She hesitated and then said, "Yes. He crashed into a train."

Hector stood up, stumbled, and saw the floor rise up to meet his face. He felt the stinging impact of the cold linoleum on his cheek. Sandra sat on the floor next to him and lifted his head onto her lap, protecting him from the stares of the crowd. He buried his face against her stomach and bit her blouse to muffle the noises coming from his mouth. After a while he felt arms lift him up and lead him to a room in the back. He lay down on a cot and sank his face into a pillow so that he could hardly breathe. He heard the door close and felt someone sit next to him on the small bed.

"I need to go home," he said.

"*Sí, lo sé.*" Sandra answered. "*Pero,* is better to rest just a while. There's nothing you can do now. *Ya mero sale el sol.* I will take you home in a little while. *Cierra los ojos un ratito.*"

Even as Hector let himself fall into the blackness, he took comfort in the warmth of her body lying next to him.

When Hector awoke, he didn't know where he was. Someone had taken off his shoes and had thrown a light white blanket over him. He sat up, and his head shrieked with a pulsating, penetrating pain.

Then he remembered: he was at El Corralito. Filiberto must be in the next room, waiting for him. He would make fun of the fact that Hector had a hangover from one gulp of beer, and they would drive home.

He walked out of the room and squinted in the early morning light pouring in from the propped-open door, probably to air the place out. In the yard outside he could see a rooster pursuing a chicken with determined steps. The rooster was so full of himself it made Hector laugh. Suddenly he was slammed by the realization that Filiberto was dead. It was just like when his father died. The day after, Hector had caught himself laughing at Taco, a dog that lived around the projects. Taco had been leaping in the air, futilely trying to catch a butterfly fluttering above his head.

It was strange how he could find things funny even after someone he loved had just died.

There were still a few people left in the bar. Solitary drinkers who seemed too tired to get up. Sandra sat alone at a table, her head resting on top of her arm. Hector stood by her side for a few seconds, then tapped her shoulder. She lifted her head slowly and then cleared her hair from her face.

"*Hola,*" she said.

"I better head home," he said. "Is there a bus I can take?"

"I'm going to take you."

Hector followed Sandra like a puppy as she got her purse, waved at the bartender, and went out to the parking lot. She opened the door of a white car whose make he did not recognize. When he got in, he felt like he had sunk into a hole in the ground. The starter cranked a few times before the pistons started pumping evenly. The motor made a dry, tapping sound as though there was no oil in the crankcase.

"Only cost me three hundred dollars," was Sandra's explanation. She shifted into second gear, and the transmission made a grinding noise, as if the car had something stuck in its mechanical throat. Sandra made a face that said, *You see what I mean?* Again Hector was struck by the way life went on as usual. He looked out the window to see only a few people out and about. A man holding a black lunch pail waited for a bus. A woman walked by, carrying a basket of bread on her head. Two small boys rode a bicycle. One sat on the handlebars while the other stood, pumping up and down on the pedals. Hector wondered if they were brothers. His headache was making him feel sick, so he rolled down the window and let the breeze hit his face.

"You okay?" asked Sandra.

"I just need to get home," said Hector. He winced at the thought of his mother and sister. "I shouldn't have been out all night."

"Filiberto want you to be there, at El Corralito last night."

"How do you know?"

"He told me he want to bring you over to meet . . . the people there."

"Why? Did he know something was going to happen?"

"He had a feeling. He want you to have a place to come. To have friends."

"Like you."

"Yes, like me." She slowed down. They were still a good fifteen minutes from crossing the Zaragoza Bridge into Ysleta, but she seemed to need more time.

"Was he your *friend,* too?" He wished immediately that he could take back the words.

Sandra stared straight ahead, her two hands tightly gripping the top of the red steering wheel. "Not like that," she said. "He was like *un hermano mayor.*"

"I'm sorry. I didn't mean anything." What was wrong with him? It was stupid to say he didn't mean to say something when clearly he did. Earlier he had cast aspersions on Gloria; now he was doing the same to Sandra. He rubbed his eyes forcefully with his thumb and forefinger.

When he opened his eyes, he saw Sandra wiping a runny nose with her wrist. She leaned over, hit the steel button of the glove compartment, and took out a tissue. She pulled the car over to the side of the road and blew her nose.

"Lo siento," she said. "I have to get you home." She shook her head as if to shake off the sorrow. Then she put in the clutch and jiggled the gear until it shifted painfully into first. She took a deep breath and said: "Filiberto thinks if something happens to him, it is good for you to have a friend."

Hector didn't understand why he felt so angry. There

was no reason for it. He didn't even know who he was angry at. The brother not more than six hours dead? Sandra, for her kindness? Himself, for being so pathetic his brother had to hire someone to be his friend? He clenched his jaw tight. He was not going to voice any of his suspicions. Once he got home, he'd never have to see her again.

In front of his house, Hector opened the car door. Sandra grabbed his arm. "Wait," she said. "This is for you." She bent her head and removed a golden chain from her neck. It got tangled in her long, black hair. "Ay," she said softly, and smiled at him. It was amazing how she could be so light and graceful even as she was full of sorrow. At the end of the gold chain was a small, oval-shaped medal. "*Es la Virgen de Guadalupe.* Filiberto gave me it for my birthday, last year. You take it now."

He studied the medal in his palm. It felt light, and still warm from her body. "He gave it to you," he said, handing it back.

"And now *I* want to give to you," she responded, closing his hand inside her two hands.

He felt himself blush. "Why?"

"*Para que te acuerdes de mí*—so you remember me."

As he walked up to his door, he was conscious of her remaining at the curb. He turned to wave good-bye, then went inside and waited for the sound of gears grating.

When he closed the door, he was struck by the quiet. Out of habit he had expected to find Mamá awake, already back from Mass and preparing breakfast. *Filiberto is dead,* he reminded himself. Without knocking first, he opened the door to his mother's bedroom. The queen-size bed took up most of the room. It was unmade and empty. On the nightstand he saw her rosary. The clock had stopped at 5:00 A.M., when the windup alarm rang itself out. He checked Aurora's room. Her bed was also empty. They must have heard about the accident.

He sat down on Aurora's bed, his mind racing with so many thoughts he didn't know which to grasp. They probably thought he'd been with Filiberto in the truck. Why the hell did he sleep over at El Corralito instead of rushing home to Conchita and Aurora? He'd left them alone when they needed him most. He remembered the feel of Sandra's body against his—it was a dream, wasn't it? Regardless, he had let himself be comforted even as his brother lay dead and his mother and sister were left alone.

"Chinga tu madre!" he swore at himself. He got up from Aurora's bed and wandered into the living room, not knowing what to do. They'd left the lights on in their rush to leave. When he reached over to turn off the table lamp, he saw a white business card near the phone. He picked it up and read it. The name on the card was Rosario Garza, the

social worker Aurora had gone to see. On impulse, he dialed the first of two numbers on the card.

A man's voice answered sleepily. "Hello."

"I'm looking for Miss Garza, please."

"She's not here," said the man on the phone. "Who's this?"

"Please, where is she? I need to talk to her. It's an emergency." He suddenly felt out of breath, as though he had run up a hill to get to the phone.

"She went to the station. Who's this?"

"Did she go this morning? Do you know if she went because of a train accident?"

"Who's this? Is this a member of the family?"

"This is Hector. My brother Filiberto died. He crashed. A train crashed into him. Where is my mother? Mamá, Aurora, *dónde están?*"

"Where are you? Are you at home? I'm going to call Rosario. They were looking for you."

"Filiberto's dead," he said flatly.

"Are you home?"

"Yes."

"Stay there. I'll get Rosario. Just wait there." Then the man hung up.

Hector went to his bedroom and stretched out on Filiberto's bed. There'd never been a time when the two of them hadn't shared a room. How could they have grown so far apart when they had spent so much time near each other? Filiberto's pillow smelled of Old Spice, the same cologne Papá had used. Inside, something opened, and pain oozed out thick and slow, like honey from a broken jar.

10

The Crows, as Hector called his mother's friends, started showing up later that morning. One by one they came and flocked around Conchita, all wailing and crying. A tired, stony-faced Aurora served them *café con leche*. Father Ochoa also came. Just before he left, he took Hector aside, blessed him, and uttered a prayer that Hector recognized as part of a sermon. "Christ knows how much you suffer. He is never far from us."

Mrs. Garza stayed for a couple of hours. She had driven Conchita and Aurora home from the hospital. It was Mrs. Garza who had prevented Conchita from looking at the remains. She convinced the authorities that a visual identification was not necessary and, in fact, impossible.

Though reluctant at first, she ended up giving Hector the full details of Filiberto's death. He needed them, hungered for them for some reason. As far as Mrs. Garza could gather from the police report, the train engineer said that a white Impala and Filiberto's Ford truck were half on, half off the railroad tracks. Side by side they drove straight toward his locomotive. At the last second, the truck tried to swerve off the tracks, but it got stuck. The Impala made it safely off.

"He said it looked like a game of chicken," Mrs. Garza told Hector. Then she peppered him with questions. "Did you know anything about this? What did Filiberto tell you last night? Did he give you any indication of what he was going to do?"

Hector tried to recall his brother's exact words at El Corralito. *I need to let the* vato *save face,* Fili had said. Did he know what was going to happen? Did he ever say he would be back? Why didn't Hector do anything to stop him?

"Are you listening to me, Hector?" They were in Hector's room, away from his mother and her friends.

"Yes," he answered listlessly.

She turned his face toward hers. "I need to know that you're not going to do anything stupid."

"Stupid?"

"You need to stay home. I don't want you going out. Your mother and sister need you now. You know that Aurora came to talk to me last week, don't you?"

"She told me." Hector didn't mean to look at her accusingly, but he did. What had she done to prevent anything? Hadn't she made things worse?

Mrs. Garza felt the silent accusation and blushed. "It was the right thing to do. Aurora's instincts were correct. I'm working on getting you moved someplace else."

"We don't want to move," Hector said stiffly.

"Okay, we can talk about that later. Right now, I need to make sure of one thing. I need to make sure that you're not going to do something stupid."

"Like what?"

"Like revenge."

"No."

"Good. We're going to find Chava. We'll arrest him for being on the tracks, and he's going to know that any move against this family will mean more trouble for him and the Discípulos. Hector? We'll talk later. Are you okay?"

Hector stared down at his bedspread. Outside the door, he heard weeping; he didn't know who it was.

Mrs. Garza left the room, closing the door behind her. He stretched out on the bed, closed his eyes, and saw his mother's face. When she had returned home from the hospital and seen Hector, many expressions had crossed her face. First there was relief. He was alive; he hadn't been in the truck with Filiberto. But then he saw something else— was it anger? Disappointment? Blame?

Aurora had been more direct.

"Where were you?" was the first thing she asked.

"I was out with Filiberto. We went out for a drink. He wanted to talk to me. He left me at the bar. Then he went to meet Chava."

"He went by himself?" It was an accusation.

"There was nothing I could do," he said defensively. It sounded weak even to him.

She shook her head and walked away.

Now, he thought, *the worst is about to begin.* The waiting, the sitting around, waiting for routine to take over again. In a few minutes he would get up and talk to people about the funeral. He felt for the bankbook in his pocket. He wouldn't let his family go into more debt over yet another funeral. They still owed money on his father's. He'd go to the savings-and-loan office and take out what they needed. Whatever was left over would be for Aurora. She was the one with a future.

He thought about the little lecture Mrs. Garza had given him. It was kind of flattering to be seen as someone capable of avenging his brother's death. Obviously she didn't know him very well. He pictured his fists pummeling Chava's face, his hands around his throat, and there was a sweet satisfaction in those images. Doing something would be better than sitting around, waiting.

He reached under the bed for his shoes. Time to face the Crows. They lived to mourn, and now they had fresh meat. He accepted their hugs, their oily concern. They made him sit down next to them on the caramel-colored sofa. His mother was nowhere in sight. She must have been lying down in her room. They offered him *café con leche* and *pan dulce*. They asked him about his night out with Filiberto. They knew about that, but not about the Discípulos. Or at least they didn't talk about it. As far as they were concerned, Filiberto was in an accident. It was a tragedy, but something like that was bound to happen to Filiberto sooner or later, given the life he led. He was a restless soul, always had been. Not like Hector, who was a good boy. Now he must pray to God to keep him strong for Conchita and Aurora, to keep what was left of the family intact.

Hector excused himself. He needed to get some air. The Crows worried about him going out by himself. Aurora came out of the kitchen and looked at him queerly. "Where are you going?"

"For a walk."

"I'm coming with you," she said.

"No," he told her firmly.

"I'm getting my sneakers," she said, ignoring him.

He opened the screen door wide and ran.

11

Hector didn't know what time it was, but the sun was still out in full force. The inside of the old church would be as cool as a cave. He had an overwhelming need to get there and say something to the bloodied Christ that hung in pain behind the altar.

The church was deserted and cold. More than a cave, it felt like being in a grave after all the mourners have left. Hector walked to the first pew and got down on the wooden kneeler. It took a few minutes for the words to rise to the surface, then they bubbled out. "All his life Fili doesn't give a shit, and the first time he cares about something, You kill him."

I have a plan, Filiberto had said. *Some plan,* thought Hector, *playing chicken on the tracks, in an old truck.* Fili had never planned anything. He'd just gone along, occasionally stirring up trouble just for the hell of it. He never had a purpose in life, and there was no purpose in his death either. This "accident" wouldn't change anything. Like always, he'd left Hector behind to pick up all the pieces. He thought he was a big *adulto,* giving Hector money, but even that was pointless, because it would be spent on another funeral. Gloria would probably go back with Chava now. "Why didn't You take Chava?" Hector asked the empty church.

He wanted to feel more—more anger, outrage, sadness, anything—but there was only a small flicker inside him, like the candle burning now in the back altar. As altar boy, he lit that candle every morning. It was supposed to signify the presence of the consecrated Host. But Hector knew there was no such presence with him. He was alone with a single, shameful thought that shone, neon white, before him: *First I wanted Papá and then I wanted Filiberto to die.*

The thought propelled him up and out the door. The church was not the place where he would find solace. The sunlight was so bright Hector stumbled in the parking lot. As he walked past the projects, he felt the dry, desert heat of El Paso bake him. Beads of sweat appeared on his upper lip and temples. His father and Filiberto were like each other. Everybody said so, and you could tell. Hector was different. He had been raised to believe that he was different. Now, however, as he strode on the dirt road toward the cotton fields, he felt that he was becoming more like his dead brother and his dead father. He was going to let this new power take him wherever it wanted to take him.

By the time he could see Gloria's house, he was soaked with perspiration. His heart pounded harder as he got closer to the white car parked under the shade of the pecan tree. An Impala that rode low to the ground.

He stopped, feeling as though he was on the edge of a precipice. If he took another step, he would fall. He could muster enough strength to turn around and head back to the apartment with its heavy curtains, the island fortified by the moat that was his father's garden, the coolness and silence of the old church, the crowded halls and classrooms of his school, where he could disappear anonymously. *Don't do anything stupid,* Mrs. Garza had said.

Then he saw the silhouette of two heads in the car's rear window. He stopped thinking. He felt a force lift him off his feet and carry him forward, the way Filiberto must have felt when he pushed the gas pedal to the floor and steered the truck straight into the oncoming locomotive. He took a hundred steps forward, but it was only one letting go, one falling—no, soaring. Then he was beside the white Impala parked under the pecan tree, and through the side window he saw them in the backseat, kissing and groping each other. Chava's left hand was on Gloria's breast, and his right hand was behind her neck, bringing her head down toward his open mouth.

Light breaks where no sun shines; where no sea runs, the waters of the heart push in their tides. This line of a poem he had memorized for English class was, of all things, what filled his head as he opened the car door and grabbed the openmouthed Chava by his hair. Hector had to try a couple of times to get ahold of his hair, because it was greasy, but when he did, he pulled so hard that some of it came out in his hand. Hector ended up with a tuft of black bristles that reminded him of a cheap paintbrush. He reached in again and managed to grab part of Chava's face. His clawing fingers found Chava's nostrils, and he used them and the open mouth to pull Chava's body out of the car. Gloria began screaming almost as soon as he opened the car door. *"No espérate!* It's not what you think!" She kept screaming as he pummeled Chava's face with his fists. Chava's nose cracked under his knuckles like a twig. In Chava's terrified pupils Hector observed, as if from a distance, his own raging figure in miniature, and it looked strangely familiar. Then Gloria was behind him, pulling him away from Chava's bloodied face, yelling that she was only trying to help, that he had it all wrong. She pulled his shoulders back so he lost his balance, and he found himself seated on the ground with his legs stretched out. This gave Chava enough time to pick himself up. Hector saw Chava wipe his bloody nose with his skinny arm, and then he saw Chava's leg move back, taking aim. Hector turned his head so as to not get hit in the face with the point of Chava's boot, but it struck his right ear. Hector was on his back, his arms outstretched. Again Hector saw himself from afar. He looked as if he was lying on top of a hill, after a picnic meal, observing the shapes of the clouds. How did that poem go? *Dawn breaks behind the eyes; from poles of skull and toe the windy blood slides like a sea.* Yeah, that was it. *The secret of the soil grows through the eye, and blood jumps in the sun.* Then what? *Above the waste allotments the dawn halts.* He curled himself up like a shrinking fetus and covered his head with his hands.

Gloria was still screaming. Hector heard other voices, too. When the kicks stopped, he opened one eye and saw that an older man was telling Chava in a tone of incongruous politeness that he was not welcome around the house anymore. At the same time he heard Gloria's mother order her to stop yelling and go inside.

"Wherever you go, I'll find you. I swear, *pendejo,* you're dead" were the last words Hector heard Chava speak. Then he heard the Impala's motor explode and the wheels shriek amid a cloud of dust.

Hector stumbled up. The man—Gloria's father?—looked lost, like he had woken up to some kind of nightmare. Gloria, red-faced, was trying to tug herself free of her mother's tight grasp.

"It's not my fault your stupid brother went and got himself killed," Gloria screamed from her mother's arms. "I didn't do anything! I hope he and your whole family go straight to hell!" Then she started sobbing.

Hector walked away. Gloria's father caught up to him, turned him around, and pointed him in the opposite direction. "Don't come back here anymore," he counseled Hector. "You're not welcome around here either."

12

If he laid his ear on the soft mud of the cotton fields, the pain diminished slightly. Water had flooded the field only the day before, so the dirt was soft and cool on his piercing ear. There were islands of pain all over his body. It felt as if his spinal column had cracked in the middle of his back. The pain in his ribs allowed him to draw only baby breaths. But it was the ear, both the outside and the canal that led into his brain, that pulsated spurts of hot hurt into his consciousness. Liquid oozed out of it, as if Chava's kick had shattered a precious vial hidden there. He tried to get up, but every time he lifted his head Hector felt as though he would fall into the white, hot sky. He dug his fingers into the black earth and held on with all his might.

Onomatopoeia. It was a term he had learned in his English class. He tried to remember the meaning of it. Maybe the kick in the ear had dislodged all kinds of words and images, and now they floated rootless in the mush that was his brain. Onomatopoeia. Onomatopopeia. Popeia. What did it mean? Something about sounds. *Slosh.* That's it. Slosh was inside his head. Slosh was an example of *onomato* whatever. It was a word that was formed from the very sound of things. *Trample.* Was that one? *Gulp?* Yeah, *gulp* could be one. *Gurgle. Gurgle. Thud.* The sound of Chava's kick on his face was a *crack.* It was definitely a *K* word. Or was it an *F* sound? Maybe a combination of both. A FUCK. Was *fuck* onomatopoeia? Is that how the word came into being? *Fuck, fuck.* The sound of bodies colliding and piercing each other? He had never fucked, but he hoped that was not the sound that would emanate from his body when he did, for *fuck* sounded more like the sound of Chava's pointed boot against his head.

"Daddy," he muttered, pushing his ear deeper into the mud of the cotton field. When he was alive, Hector had called him Papá and sometimes Dad. He only called him Daddy after he was gone. The smell of the moist earth and the feel of the soft mud reminded him of his daddy. Daddy

163

would slowly pour the brown levy water in a circle around his plants. Then he would carefully mold a crater around each one to cup the water that blessed them. And once, when a bee stung Daddy in the neck, Hector saw him pluck the bee out gently, trying to save the bee from losing its stinger and certain death. Then Daddy reached down into the flower bed, grabbed a handful of mud, and dabbed the mud as ointment on his neck.

Hector felt a hand touch his forehead. "Daddy?" He heard the sound of wind rustling through leaves. "Shhh, shhh, shh." He thought he was still asleep in the back room of El Corralito, where he had slept the night before with Sandra next to him. Sandra was telling him to let himself go into self-forgetting, pain-forgetting, guilt-forgetting, life-forgetting sleep.

When he opened his eyes, he saw the bike first and then Aurora. "What are you doing here?" he asked.

"You're in an ambulance," said Aurora. "I found you in the cotton field in front of Gloria's house."

"Ahh," he said. "Where you get the bike?"

"I borrowed it from Melinda," Aurora said. "I came looking for you."

"Shh," said a young woman dressed in light blue. "Better not to talk right now." The woman's black hair was drawn back in a ponytail, and Hector saw, as she adjusted a plastic bag that dangled above his head, that she had the arm muscles of an athlete.

"I'm sorry," mumbled Hector. He looked to Aurora for a sign of forgiveness, but she was watching the paramedic work. He hadn't said it loud enough for anyone to hear.

BOOK three

1

"I'm going to kill you."

The words circulated nightly on Hector's mental conveyor belt. Around and around went the grating sound of
his voice. Around and around went the squinted eyes, radi-
ating hatred, like the hissing flame of a welder's torch.

One afternoon Hector looked out of the library window
and saw El Topo. The air-conditioned building—the only
one at Furman—was supposed to entice kids to study, but
Hector was usually alone there. A few yards in front of him,
El Topo pretended to rake dead leaves from the cotton-
woods that shaded the library. His strokes were lazy,

uncommitted. He gathered a few leaves into a small pile and then stopped and leaned on the rake, looking around distractedly. He scratched the grass a few more times. *You can tell a lot about a person from the way they work when they think nobody's watching,* Hector remembered his father telling him.

El Topo had picked up two demerits. One more and he was out. *But here he is,* Hector thought, *still hanging on.* How? El Topo was clearly faking it, and you don't last long at Furman when you fake it. It's too hard. It's a lot easier to let yourself be placed in a juvie hall. According to X-Lax, who had been in many of them, there are places where you stay in your cell, watch TV, smoke cigarettes, eat, come out for some air, eat, go back in. You don't have to get up at six in the morning to march like a zombie, or go to classes and do homework to earn a high school degree, or spend your afternoons pulling grass out of sidewalk cracks.

In the weeks following the basketball game with El Topo and the Mayates, El Topo had waged fierce psychological warfare. He followed Hector wherever he went, his stare burning holes in Hector's back.

"That kid's trying to screw with your head," X-Lax had said one afternoon when they noticed El Topo eyeing them on the way to the toolshed.

"It looks that way," Hector had responded.

"Well, is he, Clinto? Is he getting some mental pussy from you?"

"Naah," Hector said dismissively.

"Well, remember what Díaz says."

"What?"

"No one can brain-fuck you if you don't let him."

"I never heard him say that."

"Actually, I just made it up. But it's something he mighta, coulda said."

Hector thought that not letting someone brain-fuck you was easier said than done. He wondered how long it would be before El Topo made his move, and he almost wished he would hurry up and get it over with. The waiting and the daily encounters with unrelenting hatred were a radiation slowly poisoning Hector's painfully garnered reservoir of peace.

Now Hector studied El Topo behind the protective glare of the library windowpane. What was he like without the hatred? There was something eerily familiar about him. El Topo was close enough that Hector could see his eyes. There it was, the dull, glitterless gaze of eyes unable to reflect the future. Eyes devoid of hope. Where had he seen them before?

He suddenly remembered the time when Filiberto read to his father a *National Geographic* article on wild mustangs.

Fili and Papá were sitting on the kitchen steps, cans of beer strewn by their side. After Filiberto finished reading—if you could call it that—they were both quiet, watching mustangs gallop on the private screen of their minds. Then Papá spoke.

"When the Indians of Mexico first saw the Spanish on horseback, they thought that the soldier and the horse were one."

"Yeah?" asked Filiberto.

"It must have been scary for them," continued Papá. "They had never seen a horse or a white man before. Imagine seeing someone like that—with four legs and two arms, a steel helmet, a sword."

"*Híjole.*"

"When I was young in Chiapas, my father used to take care of horses sometimes. There was this white *yegüita* he let me ride because she needed the exercise and she was gentle. She was so fast."

"*De véras?*"

"*Sí.* She was fast. I rode her bareback, with only a rope for a bridle. Then, little by little, I got her to trot, and then, after a while, we galloped like the wind. *Como el propio viento.*"

Hector, who was in the kitchen making a sandwich, moved closer to the door to hear what his father was saying.

He tried to imagine his father as a young boy on the white horse, but he couldn't.

"I know what it means to be part horse," his father continued. "When we galloped like that, I felt like I had four legs, and it was me pounding the ground with my hooves."

"You were like those Spanish soldiers," ventured Filiberto.

"You know what I felt like? What's that animal that's half horse and half person—you know, sometimes you see pictures of them."

"I forget," said Filiberto.

"Centaur," said Hector. He said it mostly to himself, but his brother and father turned around to look at him. They both broke into a grin so identical that Hector thought he was seeing an older and a younger version of the same person.

"*Un centauro.* That's what I felt like then, a centaur."

Hector wanted to join his brother and his father on the steps, but he decided against it. Then he heard his father ask, "Hector, were these centaurs for real?"

Now Hector stepped outside. "No, they were just a myth."

"A myth?" asked his father.

"A made-up story. How could a half horse, half man be real?"

173

"I believe it could happen," said Filiberto.

Sometimes it was hard for Hector to believe that his father and his brother were part of his family. They were so incredibly ignorant.

"Why couldn't it happen? Sometimes people do strange things . . . Papá, tell him," said Filiberto, laughing. "You grew up on a *rancho*."

"I don't believe this." Hector grabbed his head in desperation. "How can you possibly think that a horse and a man . . ."

His father was now laughing along with Filiberto. No wonder Hector never invited his father or brother to any school functions. Could you imagine the nonsense they were liable to say? His father grabbed him gently by the wrist and pulled him down next to them. He waited until Filiberto finished laughing and then he spoke.

"Tell me this, Hector. If these centaurs weren't real, how come we know about them?"

"Papá, someone invented them. Like La Llorona."

"Ah, no. *Un momentito*. Like La Llorona, you say?"

Hector immediately knew he had picked the wrong example.

"Everyone knows La Llorona is the spirit of a mother who lost her sons. She wanders forever looking for them."

"She's not real."

"No, Hector, no. *Estás equivocado.* I myself know people back home who have heard her cry at night by the river. Same thing with these *centauros*; why would people make them up unless they seen them?"

"I don't know."

"Do you know, Filiberto?"

"Yes," Filiberto responded without hesitation.

"Yes, I figured you would. Why, Fili?"

"Because they exist."

"There. You see, Hector? You see how your brother knows these things? He's right, you know."

"What are you talking about? Centaurs are not real. They never existed."

"When I was a young boy galloping on that mare like the sea wind, I was a centaur."

"I'd like to be a centaur, too, someday," said Filiberto.

Hector stretched his neck to look at Filiberto, expecting him to be joking. But he had a serious look on his face, as if he had just discovered a word for something he had never been able to name.

"You guys are pulling my leg." Hector stood up. "You've been drinking too much of that stuff." He pointed at the beer cans.

"Don't go yet," his father said. "Stay with us a little longer."

"I gotta go study. I have a test tomorrow." He stood up to go back inside, but his father grabbed his wrist again.

"Hector, it's not so bad to be a centaur. These *centauros*, they were not confused like most of us. They weren't men that acted like horses, or horses that wanted to be men. They knew what they were. They were happy to be centaurs. They had the best of both worlds, the brain of a man and the heart of a horse. Not like us. We're wild horses when we should be thinking, and thinking when we should be galloping with the heart of a wild horse. *Es muy difícil ser las dos cosas al mismo tiempo.* When I was a young boy on that *yegüita*, I was both. I made her fly to wherever I wanted to go, but she took me with her strength. You understand?"

Hector remembered his father's eyes as he pulled his hand away—the tired eyes of an old hauling horse on his last legs.

Hector had closed his own eyes to see the memory. When he opened them, there, pressed against the windowpane, was the contorted face of his father—and then, narrowing into focus, the hideous face of El Topo, his nose and lips flattened against the glass. Hector sprang back in horror. El Topo dangled a key in front of Hector's eyes, smirking and glaring, like the devil that often visited Hector's dreams. Then he tapped the key against the glass and rasped loud enough for Hector to hear: "I'm going to kill you."

Hector tried to grin, to look unperturbed. But he knew it was too late. El Topo had glimpsed his fear.

2

What El Topo held in his hand was the unmistakable master key to the dorms' alarm system. At 10 P.M. each night the doors were closed and the RAs turned on the alarms. The doors could still open, per fire-code regulations, but not without setting off a ring raucous enough to wake the dead. The alarm key was long and round, like the key to Aurora's roller skates.

Since the library incident, Hector had strung a fishing line across the doorless entryway to his room every night. He was embarrassed to let X-Lax know he was afraid, so he waited until he heard X-Lax sleeping, and then he strung the line taut, at the height of a person's shins. In the event that Hector dozed off, El Topo would trip and wake him up when he fell into the room.

Hector also brought a five-pound dumbbell into his room and hid it under his pillow. At night he clenched it. The feel of the cold iron comforted him. Sometimes he lifted it up and down, first one arm then the other, until he grew tired enough to sleep.

During the day he was edgy, his skin crawling with electric worms. In games with the Carnales, his jump shots ricocheted off the rim. Even when he was on outside detail and El Topo was back at school, Hector could feel his itchy presence.

His fear congealed into ice, melted with resentment, then steamed in anger. Why had El Topo come to make his life miserable just when he was beginning to sort out and deal with all that had brought him to Furman? It seemed as if someone was watching him from above, saw that he was on the verge of something resembling contentment, and dropped El Topo into his midst. Wasn't that exactly what had happened before? Things were going well, and then Filiberto had to go and hanker after Gloria. Yeah, but Filiberto had brought it on himself. And Hector had messed up in a bigger way—he admitted it—by going after Chava. Still, the El Topo punishment was disproportionately cruel and unusual.

One day Hector's trapped steam exploded. He and Sansón were working on an obstacle course on the northwest corner of the school grounds. Yoda (that's what X-Lax called Furman's diminutive and shriveled head of maintenance) had let Hector and Sansón use the backhoe to dig a trench. Hector was operating the backhoe while Sansón kept a lookout for an old, underground cesspool that Yoda said was somewhere out there. When Yoda first taught Hector how to operate the backhoe, Hector had been surprised at how adept he was at pushing pedals and jiggling levers all at once, making the machine move at his commands.

But that was before El Topo had laid siege to Hector's mind. On this day Hector's reflexes were jerky, his nerves agitated. He was convinced that El Topo was in the area, ready to attack at any moment. Hector glanced sideways to check, and in that one second of distraction the giant yellow arm of the backhoe swung and struck Sansón on the head.

"Shit!" yelled Hector, jumping off the backhoe. Sansón lay on the ground, arms and legs sprawled every which way.

"Ay," Sansón said after a few infinitely long seconds.

"Get up! Get up!" Hector screamed at him. He grabbed

Sansón by the T-shirt and began to pull him. "Get up, you stupid imbecile! It's your fault! You were too close!" He gave up trying to lift him and started shaking Sansón by the shoulders, as if loosening apples from a tree.

"I'm sorry," Sansón stuttered.

"You dumb asshole!" yelled Hector. Then, like a sound that woke him from a dream, he heard the thud of his fist on Sansón's jaw.

Startled not by pain but by Hector's angry outburst, Sansón grabbed Hector and rolled on top of him, pinning his arms to the ground.

"No," Sansón said. There was force but no hostility in his voice.

Hector clenched his jaw and pushed convulsively against Sansón's immovable mass.

"That's okay, *carnal*," said Sansón. "Push it all out. Get all that *veneno* out of you." And he anchored Hector until the last drop of rage was spent.

They walked back to the infirmary in silence. On the side of Sansón's head, Hector could see a lump the size of a small eggplant.

"I'll wait for you," said Hector when they arrived.

"I'll be okay. *Es pura roca*," said Sansón, touching his head. "You want to do the dumbbells after this?"

"I'm not sure I can lift right now," said Hector, depleted.

What he wanted to do more than anything was find a dark, hidden nook where he could crouch into a ball until the day was over. But the sight of Sansón, bashed skull and all, walking unhurriedly beside him, made him say instead, "After you get cleaned up, and if your brains didn't leak out, maybe we can do some reading."

They sat at opposite ends of the green sofa. The rec room was empty, because at that time of the afternoon no one who could be outside would be caught dead inside. Hector read from *The Old Man and the Sea,* his voice the steady monotone of someone who's not thinking about the meaning of the words.

"'He may be stronger, said the old man to himself, referring to the marlin he had hooked, but I'm smarter and I know some tricks.'"

"Too bad's the boy's not with him," Sansón interrupted.

This time, instead of ignoring Sansón's questions, Hector asked, "Why?"

"The boy coulda helped him, *verdá?*"

"I think the old man's supposed to struggle with the fish alone."

"He could of still struggled with the fish alone, but at least he'd have the boy to talk to. So he wouldn't be talking to himself *como loco.*"

"Talking wouldn't have helped him," Hector asserted.

"No, *ése,* talking to the boy woulda given him more strength. The old man wished the boy was there. He even said so in the book, *qué no?*"

Sansón paused as if he had just discovered something important. Hector saw Sansón's otherwise opaque eyes glimmer for an instant, and then he heard him say, "Maybe the old man wasn't talking to himself, maybe he was talking to the boy, pretending in his head the boy was there with him and talking to him. Maybe the thought of the boy being with him is what kept him pulling the tuna. Maybe he never gave up on the tuna 'cause of the boy."

When Sansón spoke those words, Hector finally realized who Sansón reminded him of. His brother and Sansón were completely different on the outside, but inside they had a core of something similar. Hector could not name the inner quality they shared. "Innocence" was the best he could come up with, but the word wasn't exactly right.

As Sansón paged through the book, looking for a passage he remembered, Hector looked at the patch of bare scalp on Sansón's head. Colonel Taylor, who also handled medical emergencies, had shaved a pancake-sized hole in Sansón's hair. Miraculously, no stitches had been required, and Colonel Taylor simply dabbed the gash with iodine. Now the circle of purple skin on Sansón's head seemed to Hector like an open wound through which he could see his own disgusting fear.

"*Mira,*" said Sansón, "here's the part where he wishes the boy was with him." He began to read, the syllables of each word plodding the seemingly endless journey from page to eyes to brain to tongue.

Hector's mind wandered. Was he like the Old Man being dragged to his death, or was he more like the hooked fish? If he was like the Old Man, he could just let go of the rope, admit the fish was stronger. He could tell Colonel Taylor that the kid was out to kill him. But there was something depressing about this solution. If he ratted on El Topo, he would feel like he had given up on the fish and gone home empty-handed.

If he were the fish, his only chance would be to outlast El Topo. But this solution seemed unbearable. There was no way he could continue to be dragged on El Topo's hook, thrashing in panic. The only way out for the fish was to break the line or somehow kill the Old Man.

"*Ves,*" said Sansón in the distance. "It says here the thought of not disappointing the boy gave the Old Man strength."

Hector didn't answer. He was thinking about something that lay hidden under X-Lax's mattress. It had a fake turquoise handle; on the side was a button that made a sparkling blade pop out like a jack-in-the-box. X-Lax had demonstrated its sharpness by tapping his finger softly on the point and drawing a drop of blood. "This here," X-Lax had said with the voice of experience, "is sometimes the only way to stop a brain-fuck."

3

The following Sunday was cold and rainy, so Díaz moved the
mind-training session to an unoccupied corner of the gym.
Sansón, X-Lax, and Hector found their spots and began to
lift. By now they had progressed to the point where they
didn't need to follow a prescribed routine—each could
decide the order of his own exercises. They didn't even
have to count the lifts anymore. Díaz had told them to stop
and rest their muscles whenever it felt right. If they con-
centrated correctly, they would know when to stop and
when to start up again.

The gym was noisy. Everyone at Furman, it seemed, was

there. Sometimes Hector could block out distractions by closing his eyes and adjusting his breathing to the contraction and relaxation of the lift. But that technique wasn't working today. It wasn't just the noise of balls being slapped and the shouts of kids horsing around that prevented him from focusing. There was a constant beat inside his head, as if someone had connected his brain to a boom box that played a monotonous rap: *Ain't no place to hide. Ain't no place to run. You gotta make a move. What you gonna do?*

Hector felt a tap on the shoulder. When he opened his eyes, Díaz was motioning for him to follow. They climbed the wooden bleachers that stretched, accordion-like, up the wall. From the highest level they surveyed the scene below. X-Lax was on his back, benching. Sansón skipped rope. There was a game of volleyball in the center of the gym. Groups of kids played basketball on the perimeter courts.

Díaz spoke, his gaze on the activities below. "When I first got to prison, I was on death row. I knew I had only a few months to live at most. I pled guilty of first-degree murder. I refused any appeals."

Hector had never heard Díaz speak in this tone of voice: solemn, intimate.

"I killed a young man," said Díaz, responding to the question Hector had always wanted to ask. "He was a little older than you. I didn't kill him out of anger—although I don't think I ever hated anyone as much as I hated that boy. I executed him. Even though only a few seconds went by between the time I decided to kill him and the time I pulled the trigger, it wasn't a crime of passion, it was a crime of reason."

Sansón was now squatting and rising with a barbell of weights on his back. X-Lax was doing an abdominal exercise he claimed to have invented and that, according to him, fortified his most important muscle.

Díaz continued. "When I was on death row, I met an inmate who introduced me to 'mind training with dumbbells.' One day, after we had been lifting for a while, he asked what I wanted most. I told him I wanted to face death without fear, if that was possible."

Hector looked at Díaz. It seemed as if Díaz was talking about how he, Hector, felt. Had someone told him about El Topo?

"Cortina invented a method of lifting weights with attention that he called 'the way of the jaguar.' He had read that the jaguar was the highest warrior rank of the Aztecs. The warriors were trained not to fear pain or death. The way of the jaguar was a discipline toward fearlessness."

Hector remembered El Topo's contorted face pressing against the window of the library and the fear that had gathered like a cesspool in his stomach. More than anything he wanted to be free of that feeling.

"For me, the way toward fearlessness was to go back over my life and look at the things I was afraid of. Not with blame or anger, but with the strength and calm concentration that the weight lifting had given me. The toughest part was facing the different ways I had been, was, and would always be a coward in one form or another."

Díaz's words shocked Hector at first. Then, after a moment, he felt the block of ice in his chest begin to melt. A kid below served the volleyball so high that it got stuck in the steel joints that supported the roof. Now everyone was trying to dislodge it by throwing basketballs and softballs at it.

Díaz was unperturbed by the noise below. "Eventually, with Cortina's help, I was able to face my execution without fear. That's when I asked for clemency. I asked to be allowed to live not because I was afraid to die, but because I was full of regret over all the hurt I caused. I wanted a chance to die without regret. I was fortunate to be given a little more time to make it up to life, to others."

Now the kids below came up with another idea. A small, agile boy named Memín clambered halfway up the climbing rope. X-Lax, who had abandoned his special sit-ups, swung him toward the volleyball. Armed with a broom handle, Memín tried to poke the volleyball loose. The sight of Memín dangling on top of the rope and X-Lax swinging him below reminded Hector of a circus act.

Hector saw Díaz grinning broadly and realized that, incredibly, illogically, Díaz was a happy man. This man spending his life in prison was beaming with enjoyment.

"I guess we're not going to do any mind training today . . . with the dumbbells, anyway." Díaz winked at Hector. He waited for Hector to speak.

Hector was surprised at how effortlessly his words came out. "I don't want to be a coward." Then, after a long pause, he added, "Anymore."

Díaz smiled knowingly. "You know what Cortina told me when I said almost those same exact words?"

Hector shook his head.

"He said there was nothing wrong with being a coward as long as you didn't act like one." The memory made Díaz laugh.

Was that the first time Hector had seen him laugh out loud?

After the sound of his laughter drifted away, Díaz took a deep breath, like someone gathering the strength to part with a cherished secret. When he spoke, his tone was soft. "I know that there's something disturbing you. Some decision you need to make. I know it's something heavy and pressing. We could talk specifics if you'd like. But if we did, I would only say what I already said to you today. Maybe I would add this: true courage—true fearlessness—comes from love."

"Love?" Hector's image of love did not jibe with his image of courage.

"The love I'm talking about," said Díaz, guessing what was going through Hector's mind, "is not soft—it's hard. It means accepting responsibility for the other person's suffering and well-being. It means helping each other, regardless of how we feel, because we're all connected."

They turned their heads in time to see Memín, propelled by a death-defying swing from X-Lax, pry the ball loose. As the ball dropped, the gym filled with the jubilant sound of clapping and yelling. Memín and X-Lax began to bow and wave with exaggerated gestures, soaking up the cheers.

"See?" said Díaz, pointing at Memín and X-Lax. "You can't do it alone."

It was pouring even worse when Hector returned to his room. X-Lax had gone on cafeteria duty, and everyone else was in the TV room watching the Dallas Cowboys play the New York Giants. Hector pulled out the chair to his desk and sat. For once his mind wasn't spinning with images of El Topo. He felt calm but empty, strong but alone. He closed his eyes and repeated as many of Díaz's words as he could remember. They were unequivocal, clear, yet they still needed deciphering, like a code. But a code to what? Hector had wanted someone to tell him what to do, but Díaz hadn't offered any specific advice. Or had he?

True courage, true fearlessness, comes from love. How can that be? Anger had always been Hector's one and only source of courage. Love? For whom? For El Topo? Even under Díaz's definition—no, *especially* under Díaz's definition of the word—it was impossible. The prolonged heat of his loathing had scorched his insides dry. No love of any kind could grow in there. For that matter, whom had he ever loved?

He stared at the bottom drawer of his desk. He braced himself before opening it. The white envelope was under the unused blue pajamas. The paper shook in his hands as he opened it.

Hey, Bumhead,

By the time you open this, you'll be at your new school. Knowing you, you're probably going to sneak out tomorrow morning without saying good-bye, so I'm writing this and hiding it in your suitcase. It's better if I write anyway. Every time we talk these days we end up pissed. You think I blame you for Fili's death, but I don't. I'm glad you didn't go with him to meet Chava, and I know there was nothing you could do to stop him. Fili was Fili. I wish I could convince you. What I really wish is I could kick

your butt and say wake up, Hector. Don't pass this up.
It probably doesn't seem like it now, but this is a bendición, *as Mamá says. You're out of here, and you're in a*
place where you can finally be Hector. Don't worry about
us. Mamá will be fine in a couple of weeks once she knows
you're safe, and I got lots of plans. Don't forget to write,
jerko.

Tu carnalita,
Aurora

4

Hector listens to the sounds of the night. He feels the vibra-
tions from X-Lax's fan. X-Lax changes positions in his bed
and sighs. Outside a cricket chirps with steady and ceaseless
rhythm. Hector turns up the volume of his hearing aid as
high as it will go. He waits motionless until he hears the
steady breath of X-Lax's sleep.

He grabs the flashlight and X-Lax's knife from under his
pillow and descends from his bunk. Barefoot, he walks out
of the room. There is no fishing line across the door tonight.

The hall is lit by dim orange lights, in case someone
needs to find their way to the bathroom. He walks to Ron-

nie the RA's room, the last doorway down the hall. He listens to make sure Ronnie is asleep, then enters and feels for the desk. Hector opens the drawer and immediately finds the master key to all the dorms. The ease with which he finds it confirms the sense that all of this, all that happens this night, is meant to happen.

He disables the alarm, then pushes down the steel bar on the door to the outside. It creaks and he freezes for a long moment, but Ronnie doesn't stir. Hector opens the door just enough for his body to fit through. Once outside, he locks the door and reactivates the alarm. Should someone need to enter or exit, they won't notice anything amiss. He carefully places the master key in the pocket of his shorts.

He takes a deep breath and looks at the stars. It has been a long time since he's been out at this hour of night. He starts to walk. There's no need for the flashlight. The light of the moon and the spotlights on the sides of the buildings are enough to guide his way. He feels a stone pierce the sole of his foot and suddenly remembers that Filiberto was barefoot when he went to retrieve Hector's basketball from the Discípulos. If Fili could have foreseen all that unraveled from his one act, would he have continued toward it?

Hector circles around Dorm D once to make sure that everyone inside is asleep. The key enters easily into the lock and deactivates the alarm. The door makes a loud click.

After a while he steps inside. The layout of every dorm is exactly the same, so he knows the location of Room 5, sixth door on the left. He enters.

El Topo is sleeping face-up on the bottom bunk with his mouth wide open, as if he's having trouble sucking enough air to fill his lungs. His legs are sprawled crooked on the bed, and he's wearing only the Furman regulation gray gym shorts. There is no roommate in the top bunk. In a few days it will be filled by someone from Furman's long waiting list. The time to act is now or never. But Hector does not feel the need to rush. He is strangely calm. The image of Sansón quietly lifting comes to mind and gives him strength.

He turns on the flashlight. The sound of the desk chair scraping the linoleum startles El Topo awake. Hector recognizes the momentary look of terror on El Topo's face.

"What the fuck!"

"Shhh." Hector lifts his index finger to his lips. He pulls the chair closer to the bed, his eyes fixed on El Topo's. He lets their eyes adjust to the light of the flashlight shining on the floor. He places the unopened knife on the linoleum inside the flashlight's circle of illumination and waits until he sees a look of understanding on El Topo's face. Then he says, "I could have stuck a knife in you while you slept."

"Do it now, *puto*. Give it your best shot."

"Ask yourself, Why didn't I do it?"

"What the fuck are you talkin' about, *ése*?"

"Maybe you think I'm afraid. Do I look scared to you? You've been around. You know when a *vato*'s scared and when he's not."

El Topo furrows his eyebrows.

"I'm not going to kill you when you're asleep or when you're not looking. But I can't let you kill me either. That wouldn't be right. So we have a situation here."

"Get the fuck outta here, *ése*. I'll fuck you when it fucking pleases me."

"Keep it down. You're gonna wake up the RAs."

"The RAs suck my *verga*," El Topo says, lowering his voice to a loud whisper.

"Tell me something," says Hector quietly. "What happens to you if you don't kill me?"

"Quit the bullshit, *pendejo*. You think you're so fucking smart."

"No, man, I don't. If we go at it, maybe we'll both get in a few good hits. But then they'll kick us both out of here. And you know they're not going to send us to the same place. They're not that stupid. So where does that leave you and your mission? And, if somehow you manage to kill me or I you, either way the rest of our lives are shit."

El Topo rubs his eyes with two fingers, like a person trying to climb out of a bad dream.

"You could try to sneak into my dorm some night," Hector continues. "You have the key."

El Topo squints, as if trying to imagine it.

"But there's something *cobarde* about sticking someone while they're sleeping, *verdá?* I don't think you're a coward."

El Topo sits up. His sight is lost for a moment in the darkness. Then, recovering, he says snidely, "That's right, *putito*. I got more *huevos* than you'll ever have."

"Yeah? I used to think having *huevos* was the same as not giving a shit about what happens. *No sé.* I'm not so sure anymore. What do you think?"

Hector waits for an answer. When none is forthcoming he says, "Anyway, I don't see too many ways out of this situation. If you come up with something, let me know. As for me, I'm through with you. I'll be watching out for you, but I'm not going to worry about you. Now you know."

"Get outta here," El Topo blurts with a dismissive wave of his hand. "I'll deal with you when I'm good and ready."

Hector nods to let El Topo know he understands. He picks up the knife with his thumb and finger, as if he were picking up a sleeping lizard, and steps out backward, slowly.

Outside, the stars are imbued with a pale, yellow hue. Hector thinks they would be shining the same way if he had killed El Topo. What do they care about the childish games people play? He walks back to the dorm like someone walking home at the end of a long day of hard physical labor. The day's work has been done and done well. But there are hundreds and hundreds of days just like it still to come. There's no way to rid himself of El Topo, or his past. He'll have to live with both.

Back in his bunk, he hears X-Lax ask, "Did you croak him?"

"I thought you were asleep."

"Two years here and the only night I wake up to take a dump, I find my roomie gone."

"No, I didn't croak anybody."

"You weren't, like, doing it with another kid, were you?"

"No."

"Good. I'd be sorely disappointed if you, Clinto, of all people, liked going in the back door."

"Good night."

"Hey, Clinto?"

"Yeah."

"You're not gonna string your fishing line tonight?"

"You knew about that?"

"Actually, tonight's the second night I had to take a dump in the middle of the night. The other time I tripped on your wire and nearly cracked my ONE and ONLY."

"You don't have to worry about the wire. It's not going up anymore."

"I guess you won't be needing the knife either, huh?"

"Did you think I'd use it?"

"Let's just say that's a decision you had to make all by your very lonesome."

"Here, it's all yours."

"Hey, Clinto?"

"I need to get some sleep, X-Lax."

"I'm thinking that maybe I'll get my Bobbie to meet me by the back fence some night."

"I wouldn't do that. The fence has an alarm."

"I'm thinking that I wouldn't have to climb the fence, that I can love my Bobbie right through one of the chinks, without setting off the alarm. Hey, Clinto, Bobbie has a friend, Yvette, who's HUMONGOUS. We could double date. Wanna see her picture?"

"No, I don't. Listen, X-Lax. I took the risk of stealing the key from Ronnie and going out at night because it was important. There was no other way to let the kid know I wasn't afraid of him. But what you're proposing to do is silly. The benefits don't outweigh the risk."

"That's where you are sooo, sooo wrong, Clinto. Bobbie's benefits—any woman's benefits—are ENORMOUS. A taste, just a tiny taste outweighs all risks known to mankind. Clinto? You awake? Is that you snoring? That's so rude, dude. I'm sharing with you the deepest secret of life, and you fall asleep. Oh, Clinto, Clinto, you have so much to learn about the one and only thing that matters: the sweet nectar of the gods."

5

A group of thirty Furman students waited for the rented school bus to arrive. It was part of Colonel Taylor's "Furman is a privilege" philosophy to make sure that every student visited a "real" juvenile detention center or an adult prison at some point during his stay. "You need to see how bad it could be to realize how good you have it," Colonel Taylor had declared during one of his Sunday lectures. His lectures were often about the reasons behind a Furman procedure or program—"marching builds team spirit" kind of thing—but no one was ever convinced by the Colonel's justifications for the school's tortures.

It was a different story when it came to the prison trips. Kids who participated, although they never admitted it, understood the moral behind the visits.

El Topo took the empty seat behind Hector on the bus. Hector made a mental note of El Topo's location while keeping his eyes fixed on the scenery outside the window. In the days that followed his nighttime encounter with El Topo, Hector had come to believe that El Topo would not sneak up on him, either at night or from behind. It was as if Hector's visit had thrust upon El Topo an honor code he had to accept.

The hour-long trip was loud with joking and boasting about prison experiences. But the volume decreased as they approached the penitentiary. They turned off the main highway and traveled down a road that became more desolate with every passing mile. Run-down houses with mangy dogs and the remains of gutted cars in their front yards turned into shabby house trailers rusting permanently on cement blocks. Even these disappeared before the complex came into view.

Three rows of wire fences kept the Furman students from getting a good look at the red-brown buildings that adjoined one another like a drawn-out game of dominoes. The prison was a one-story, flat structure that looked as if it had been dropped onto the ground in one piece. The only height came from the guard towers that shot up, concentration camp–like, from every corner. Hector looked for a basketball court or a baseball field or any other sign of human life, but there was none.

A giant section of the fence miraculously opened when the bus pulled up to it. Everyone on the bus turned around to see the fence close and bolt shut behind them. Then they waited in the bus, trapped between two rows of fence, until a guard wearing a black baseball cap approached and told them where to park. The students followed him through the main entrance and into a brightly lit room, where they sat on yellow plastic chairs. The room seemed to be designed for prisoners, not visitors. There were no windows, and the two doors looked as if they were forever closed. Hector saw in the faces of the other students the same apprehension he was feeling.

Finally, a woman dressed in a dark skirt and white shirt told them, in a robotlike voice, what to expect: "You have entered a medium-security prison." The Furman students looked at one another as if to say, *If this is medium, then what's maximum like?*

"You have special permission to visit the cell of your host inmate," she droned on. "In order to ensure the safety of those proceeding beyond the visitors' lounge, all of the inmates have been remanded to their cells for the duration of the visit, which is to last no longer than one hour. Because of this tour, the inmates had to give up their usual hour of outside time. Consequently, some of them are none too happy. Under no circumstances are you to engage in conversation with anyone other than the inmate you have been assigned to. And one more thing, a piece of personal advice." She seemed to come alive here. "Take a good look around, because this, or worse, is where you could end up."

They followed her single file down a hallway into a big locker room with wooden benches. Hector could see urinals and curtainless shower stalls through a side opening. The woman told them to strip down to their underwear and socks and put on the orange jumpsuits in front of them, then she left to give them some privacy. Five minutes later she returned to lead them through another hallway to a red, iron door. The woman signaled at a camera and waited for the door to be opened from the inside. They entered a tunnel-like room that held a huge metal detector. One by one they stepped through the machine.

When all had been searched, a glass door at the end of the tunnel opened with an electronic *swoosh*. They entered a waiting area that resembled a hospital operating room, with stainless-steel tables and chrome stools bolted to the white floor.

Ten minutes later a small group of convicts in dark blue

jumpsuits, each one accompanied by a guard, entered. It took a minute for Hector to recognize Díaz among them. Díaz greeted X-Lax, Hector, and Sansón and asked them to follow him. As they left the room, Hector saw two convicts approach El Topo. They didn't look enthusiastic about his visit.

Díaz and his guard took Hector, X-Lax, and Sansón through a maze of metal doors with thick glass windows, through which eyeballs glared at them. Díaz had a cell all to himself, containing a bunk covered tightly with a faded gray blanket, a combination sink and seatless toilet, a bookcase, a chair, and a desk. The bookcase was completely filled, and there were books stacked high in piles on the floor, making it almost impossible to walk. The desk held a manual typewriter, a stack of legal folders, four sandwiches of unusually white bread, and a banged-up tin pitcher filled with a dark liquid. The walls of the cell were bare except for a wooden crucifix that looked as if it had been hand-carved. Hector hadn't thought Díaz was a religious type.

When they were all seated—on the bed, the chair, and the floor—Díaz passed around the sandwiches and filled their glasses with the dark liquid, which became murky red when poured and tasted like a mixture of raspberry Kool-Aid and laundry detergent. The guard stood outside the cell, his back to them.

After they finished eating, Díaz asked, "You have any questions about prison life?"

Sansón and Hector looked at X-Lax, hoping he would say something, but his tongue was busy trying to remove a piece of bread that was stuck to his palate.

"How long do you have to stay here?" Hector finally asked.

"All my life," answered Díaz without any hesitation or hint of emotion.

"I mean, when are you eligible for parole?"

"I'm not," said Díaz. "One of the conditions of having my death sentence commuted was that there would be no parole."

Sansón asked incredulously, "You're gonna be here until you die?"

"Maybe not in this cell or this prison, but one like this, yes."

"Man," groaned Sansón. He looked like a two-year-old determined not to cry.

"But suppose you do your time good and rehabilitate and all. I mean, they can change their minds, right? Later on? And let you out?" Sansón uttered the words as best he could.

"I don't think so," said Díaz. Hector looked for signs of bitterness or regret on Díaz's face, but it was as blank as the bread they had tried to chew.

"Can I ask you a personal question?" asked X-Lax, emerging victorious from his battle with the bread. Hector and Sansón rolled their eyes at each other with mock dread.

"Go ahead."

"How do you live without . . . women?" Hector could tell that X-Lax had substituted the noun at the last second.

Díaz wrinkled his forehead in deep thought. Apparently the question did not sound as stupid to him as it had to Hector.

"For some, sex is available in prison, in different forms. Others just live without it. Each prisoner has his own way of dealing with it. The harder part is how to live without women, without the presence of a woman, without the soul of woman. It's a loss. There's no other word for it. One of the biggest losses imposed by prison life."

"Man," X-Lax exclaimed, "I'd kill myself."

"That's always an option," said Díaz.

"You ever think about it?" asked Hector. The question flew out of his mouth before he realized it.

Díaz gazed at him a long time before speaking. "No," he finally said. "I like it here."

Hector looked around the cell. There was something comical about Díaz "liking" the six-by-eighteen universe where he was slated to live out his days. But there had been no sarcasm in his voice. Then, in an instant, Hector understood that "here" encompassed more than the room.

"I've worked hard at liking it here," Díaz said with a laugh that was infectious.

"Where do you lift?" asked Sansón. Díaz reached under the bed and took out two twenty-pound dumbbells and a jump rope.

"Most of the time I work out outside. But sometimes I use these in here. The jump roping I do out in the hall."

"You get to move around?" asked Sansón.

"This wing houses a bunch of old lifers like me who have shown through the years they aren't a danger to anyone. We get a little more legroom. In the other wings there're more restrictions."

"You ever have trouble, you know, with other guys?" X-Lax asked, casting a sidelong glance at Hector.

Díaz acknowledged the question's relevance with a nod. "This place has its own unwritten rules. I obey them to the extent that I can. I'm fortunate to have a couple of good friends who watch out for me; the others respect me enough to leave me alone. I show respect, too, and try to help people whenever it makes sense. It's just like your place, no?"

X-Lax, Sansón, and Hector all nodded.

"You read all these books?" asked Sansón in astonishment.

"Yes. Some of them a couple of times."

Hector, who was sitting closest to the bookcase, squinted at the titles. He saw that the books were arranged in alphabetical order.

"You know any of these?" Díaz asked Hector.

"I started reading this one, once," said Hector, pulling out the *Bhagavad-Gita*.

"Do you remember what it's about?"

Hector absently stroked the book's cover, recalling the night Filiberto invited him to go out for a drink. He was still remembering when he responded to Díaz: "It's about this warrior who's afraid to go into battle because he'll have to fight members of his family. So Krishna, his charioteer, who's really the incarnation of God, convinces him that it's okay to go into battle."

"Good," said Díaz. Hector heard admiration in his voice.

"Wow, *ése*," uttered Sansón.

"That's my roomie," said X-Lax proudly.

"It helps," Díaz said quietly, "to think of the battlefield as the mind. The dialogue between Krishna and Arjuna, the warrior, is a dialogue that takes place within ourselves, and the enemy are all the cherished illusions we avoid battling. In the process of urging Arjuna to fight, Krishna explains why life is worth living."

"How to pursue happiness," said Hector absentmindedly.

"Yes," said Díaz with a gleam, "that's right. Krishna reveals to Arjuna where and how to find happiness in its true form."

"Is that where it comes from—the mind training that we do—from these books?" asked X-Lax.

Díaz smiled. "Yes, that book is about a kind of mind training. Maybe not with dumbbells, but mind training nevertheless."

Hector flipped through the pages and saw passages underlined in pencil. The lines were perfectly straight, as though they had been drawn with the help of a ruler. *That's the way I used to study,* Hector thought.

Hector could hear the muffled sound of a distant television set. He felt strangely at ease in the cell, probably because Díaz was so at home here that he was finally allowing the three of them to see who he really was.

"What's supposed to happen to your brain after you weight-lift like that for a long time? Does it get smarter?" Sansón asked.

Hector looked at X-Lax, expecting him to make one of

his typical smart-ass comments, but X-Lax was riveted on Díaz, as if he, too, was desperate to hear the answer.

Díaz said, "When you set your mind on doing the same thing over and over again every day, something does happen. Your will is strengthened. And the attention you use to lift the dumbbells becomes a force you can control, an awareness that you can direct to other areas of your life."

Hector smiled slightly as he thought that Sansón had, without even knowing it, attained that kind of control and awareness.

Díaz continued, now addressing X-Lax and Hector. "Eventually we recognize that there is a self inside of us who is capable of controlling our body's movements. There is someone who asks the arm to lift a dumbbell even when it hurts; there is someone who tells the arm to stop and rest. Becoming aware of this self is a giant step. Before we act, before we move our body or utter a word, we must first consult with this self."

Díaz paused. With a narrowing of his eyes he asked if they wanted to hear more. Hector nodded.

"Then there's the stage when we realize that we are not our body, or our thoughts, or our emotions. Whoever we are is something separate. Just as we can direct the arm to move, we can decide to let go of unwanted thoughts and emotions. They go away with our watching. They move on."

In the silence that followed, Hector was pierced by the memory of those times when he had wished his father, his brother, dead.

Díaz turned his gaze on Sansón. "Some people say that after training for a long, long while, the flashlight turns into a light as bright as the sun. As for me, it's sufficient that the dumbbells help me live. They help me live *here*." Díaz spread out his arms to indicate the cell, then he folded his hands in his lap.

It seemed as though only a few minutes had passed when the guard turned around and said that visiting time was over. Sansón pulled Díaz to his chest and gave him the Furman salute, chest to chest, fists on the back. After a moment's hesitation, Díaz pressed his fists against Sansón's back. X-Lax then took Díaz's hand and gave him a complicated handshake consisting of various holds and finger locks, which Díaz did his best to follow. When it was Hector's turn to say good-bye, Díaz removed the *Bhagavad-Gita* from the bookcase again. He placed the book in Hector's hands.

"My gift to you," he said solemnly.

"Are you sure?" Hector blurted, even though he could see that Díaz wanted to give it to him. "It has your underlining." Hector held the book delicately, like a gift he felt unworthy to receive.

"You'll see," said Díaz, smiling, "I underlined the same passages you would have."

"Thank you," Hector was barely able to utter. A knot clenched his throat.

When Hector, X-Lax, and Sansón got out to the prison parking lot, all of the other kids were already seated on the bus. El Topo was sitting by himself in the back. Hector hesitated briefly, then decided to sit next to him. El Topo didn't even bother to look up.

The drive back to Furman was like riding inside a hearse. The only sounds came from El Topo, who, halfway through the trip, pushed his way past Hector and ordered the driver to stop the bus. El Topo barely had time to step out before he retched a foamy, pink and white liquid. When he finally finished spewing out all that was inside of him, he wiped his mouth with his sleeve and climbed back on the bus. He had sprayed his shoes and pants with vomit, and now the whole bus stank with it. Kids grimaced and slid open windows as he walked by. El Topo sat down next to Hector again, trying to look as if nothing had happened.

"What's wrong with you?" Hector asked.

"Those *putos* must've put something in that shit they made me drink."

"Why would they do that?"

"You don't know fuck, do you? They give you something

to feel sick so you'll get scared and shit in your pants when they lay their big, tough words on you. Words don't scare me. I eat words and shit them."

"What the hell's the matter with you? You want to spend your life in a place like that?"

"I've been in worse shit holes," El Topo said, his eyes narrowing, as if he was remembering. Then, stopping himself, he snarled, "I ain't through with you either, *puto*."

"Just let go of it, *ése*. Why do you keep torturing yourself? It's not worth it."

El Topo grabbed Hector's T-shirt by the collar. With sour breath he hissed in Hector's face, "What if I don't want to let it go? What if it's personal, *ése?*"

El Topo sounded like Chava way back then. Hector sat still until, with a final tug, El Topo released his grip.

"Man," said Hector with a smile, "you got puke all over your chin."

6

Yoda asked Hector and Sansón to finish digging the trench they had started the day Hector whacked Sansón on the head with the backhoe. This time, though, instead of the keys to the backhoe, Yoda handed them a pickax and shovel. Yoda was like all the other Furman staff—once you messed up, you had to work twice as hard to regain their trust.

"It won't happen again," Hector pleaded. Without the backhoe, they were looking at a whole day of backbreaking work under the sweltering sun.

"No can do," Yoda said, shaking his head firmly. "Anyways, there's an old septic tank somewheres out there, and I wouldn't want the backhoe to hit it."

And, as if digging under a ninety-eight-degree sun wasn't enough, Yoda also saddled them with El Topo.

"We'll get it done faster if you don't make us work with him," Hector objected. "The kid doesn't know how to work."

"I know it," said Yoda. "That's why I'm putting him with you two."

"Where is he, then?" Hector asked, resigned.

"I told him to go up there and get started," said Yoda. Then he looked at Hector and added, "Don't go killing anybody, now."

Hector and Sansón ambled over to the obstacle course. In the distance they could see El Topo standing next to his pickax, staring at the ground. Hector usually looked forward to working outside, even when the work involved hard physical labor. But today he dragged his feet as if he were heading to his execution. The pace was too slow even for Sansón.

"Come on, let's get started before it gets too hot," Sansón urged.

"Look at him standing up there doing nothing," Hector complained.

"El Topo's strong," Sansón observed. "Maybe we can finish before noon."

"It's going to take us longer if we have to get him to help out," Hector said dryly.

"Hey, Hector?"

"What?"

Sansón stopped and turned to look Hector in the eyes. "You think El Topo's mean, or just stupid?"

"I don't know. Why?"

"If you're just stupid, like me, you have a chance of changing. If you're mean, *es más difícil.*"

"You're not as stupid as you look," quipped Hector.

"No, man, I am." Sansón either didn't catch or didn't acknowledge Hector's humor.

They were now leaning on their picks and shovels, their gaze directed at El Topo. "Which do *you* think he is?" Hector asked.

"He's mean," Sansón said with authority, as if he had already spent a lot of time considering the question. "But he could be mean 'cause he's stupid, not 'cause he likes being mean. You know what I'm saying?"

"No," said Hector. "Explain further." Lately, Hector enjoyed asking Sansón to articulate his thoughts. It was like watching the gears inside of a clock—one with a couple of parts missing.

The words came slowly. "When you're mean because you're stupid, you act mean 'cause you think you have to.

Like when you think someone's out to get you, or someone did something to you. When you're mean because you like being mean, there's no reason for it. You just like the way it makes you feel."

"Wow!" said Hector, impressed. Maybe the reading was having an effect on Sansón after all. "That's not bad."

Sansón beamed with pride. He went on, apparently on a roll. "El Topo, maybe he's after you for a stupid reason. Like he's afraid of you. Or he thinks you're stuck-up 'cause you're smart and he feels put down. Maybe *te tiene envidia.*"

Hector lifted the pick and started walking, with Sansón following. El Topo had cut a long, skinny branch from the willow tree and was peeling off its leaves, turning the branch into a whip. From day one Hector had been certain that El Topo was sent by the Discípulos to kill him. There was no other reason for El Topo to threaten him. But what if Hector was wrong? What if the kid was just stupid, as Sansón said, and El Topo was only reacting to something about Hector?

"We can find out if he's mean or stupid," Sansón said, inspired.

"How?" Hector was intrigued.

"We can be nice to the kid. If he's just stupid, his meanness will go away sooner or later."

Hector started laughing. "I don't think it works that way."

"*Es verdad, carnal.* Take it from me. Before I came here, I was one mean, angry *vato.*"

Hector stared at Sansón in disbelief. He couldn't picture any meanness in Sansón, ever. Then again, there was something about Sansón that reminded Hector of his brother, and Hector vividly recalled the streaks of cruelty that had occasionally burst from Fili.

"It's easy, man," Sansón said encouragingly. "All you have to do is pretend to be nice to him."

"Speaking of stupid, that'll never work," Hector declared. "The kid's just plain mean."

Nevertheless, when they reached the spot where they were to start digging, Sansón called out to El Topo as if he were a long-lost friend. "Come on, *ése,* if we hurry, we can finish before noon."

Hector was surprised to see El Topo drop the willow branch and head toward them, his gait like that of someone who has reluctantly agreed to grace inferiors with his presence. The three of them stood looking at the excavation Hector had done with the backhoe. The hole was only a little bigger than a grave.

Hector spoke first. "We have to go that same depth and width another fifty feet."

"Go for it," El Topo said, staring at Hector with menacing and shifty eyes. Hector realized that once he was in the trench, the back of his head would be an easy target for El Topo's pick. The thought elicited more annoyance than fear. Part of the reason was Sansón's comforting presence. But there was something else, too, something new about the way he saw El Topo. He reminded Hector of the rattler he and Sansón once encountered on outside detail. Even after Sansón had cut off its head, the dismembered snake kept coming after him. He had moved cautiously away from the twitching body, but he had no longer been threatened by it.

"We'll need to take turns digging since only one person fits in the hole," said Hector, ignoring El Topo.

"This is bullshit," said El Topo. "How long are we supposed to be out here?"

"Until it's done. That's what Yoda said," Sansón responded. "It's not so bad." He jumped in, pick in hand, and grabbed a handful of soil. *"Está blandita la tierra."*

Sansón swung the pick over his head and was about to strike when Hector called out, "Wait, wait. We need to be fair so that no one gets stuck doing more work than anybody else. We'll take turns. You do fifty swings with the pick, then you"—Hector nodded toward El Topo—"go in and dig out the loose dirt. Then I'll go in and do fifty hits, and you'll dig out, and so on." El Topo had a look of thoughtful suspicion on his face. "I'm giving you the easy job," said Hector. "Shovel work is easier than pick work."

"How about I dig your grave?" said El Topo. "The *vato* who digs does the most work. You think I'm stupid?"

Hector and Sansón tried hard to contain their laughter. "No, man, honest, at least *I* don't think you're stupid," said Hector with a meaningful look at Sansón. "You're right. The person who digs ends up doing twice as much work as the others. Sansón, you dig. But I got to tell you, you've got to be careful with the pick. You could hit big rocks, or—"

"Shut your hole already!" muttered El Topo.

"Okay, I'll start things off." Hector swung the pick at the side of the trench fifty times, counting out loud. Then Sansón went in and shoveled out the dirt that Hector had loosened. Hector counted each shovelful of brown, moist lumps, like the soil Papá had brought from the levy to fill the garden around their apartment.

"Forty-two," said Hector when Sansón had finished digging out his dirt.

"Twenty-eight," he announced when Sansón finished digging out El Topo's dirt.

El Topo did not let on that he was paying attention to

the counts. But Hector winked at Sansón when El Topo flung off his shirt and attacked the side of the trench with angry zeal.

Hector stopped counting. "I smell something," he said, sniffing the air.

"You didn't count the last two, *puto*," El Topo said.

"It smells like gas," warned Hector. "Don't go so hard—maybe there's a gas line."

"You see that?" El Topo pointed at a red brick sticking out of the ground. "That's your face, *pendejo*."

El Topo heaved the pick high above his head, paused, and with a thrust that seemed propelled by a lifetime of unavenged humiliation, he drove the pick's steel point through the brick. Pieces of red clay exploded in all directions. There was a noise like a giant walnut cracking. As El Topo struggled to dislodge the pick from something holding it in the ground, the smell of ammonia filled Hector's nostrils. Then there was a sudden rumble, and before Hector could stretch out his hand, El Topo had been swallowed by a foul-smelling hole in the earth.

A few seconds later, two black hands emerged from the oily muck. Sansón and Hector, on their bellies at the edge of the trench, each grabbed a hand and pulled until a head popped up, spitting and cursing.

"Shit! You *cabrones* knew about this!" El Topo yelled as Hector and Sansón dragged him out.

"It smells like rotten eggs," Sansón announced.

"It's the septic tank. The cement must have given way and crumbled," Hector explained.

El Topo tried to wipe his eyes, but his sludge-covered fingers only made matters worse. "Give me my shirt," he commanded.

Hector put the clean shirt into El Topo's muddy hands. "I tried to tell you," he said. "I tried to tell you to go easy."

"Let's go back to the toolshed and hose you down, *carnal*," Sansón said sympathetically. "You can get sick from swallowing *mierda*."

El Topo ignored Sansón. "You're dead," he mouthed at Hector. He wasn't uttering a threat, he was stating a fact. Then he turned around and waddled off like an oil-covered duck.

As they watched him go, Hector said, "Think we were nice enough to him, Sansón?"

They fell on the grass, laughing as they tried to hold their noses.

7

It was Hector's idea to invite El Topo to play with the Carnales. "There are only five of us. Without him, we won't have any relief. The Mayates will run us ragged." They turned around to look at El Topo sitting by himself on the wooden bleachers.

"*Estás loco,*" was Tulito's response.

"We put him in just long enough for us to get a breather when we need one. We won't be able to keep up with them otherwise. It's hard enough to play those guys when we're full strength."

"Let's go, ladies," one of the players from the Mayate

team yelled at them. "Don't y'all be shy, now. Come get your piece of humble pie!"

"Fine," said Tulito. "You ask him if you want. But he better keep his mind on the game."

Furman kids began to gather around the court to watch the afternoon game. Hector walked over to the bleachers reluctantly, wondering whether he had made the right decision. He had been trying to ignore the revulsion he felt toward El Topo, as if El Topo were permanently covered with the contents of the septic tank.

El Topo watched him approach with a fixed glare. Hector forced himself to sound natural. He remembered Sansón's words: *All you have to do is pretend.*

"We could use your help, *ése*. We only have five guys. The rest of the *vatos* are on a field trip."

El Topo stretched his legs and looked at Hector as from a mountaintop.

"The guys asked me to ask you," Hector lied. "We could use some muscle on the inside."

Hector waited for a response, but El Topo did not move. His arms spread out, his dark legs sprawled over the bleachers, he seemed like a toad whose only sign of life came from an almost imperceptible movement of the eyes. Hector shrugged his shoulders as if to say, *I tried.*

He was halfway down to the court when he heard El Topo yell after him.

"Hey!" El Topo descended the bleachers ever so slowly, like an old man riddled with arthritis. "I'm not subbing for anyone. I start."

"Go ahead and start. But you have to come out when it's your turn to come out. That's the way the game is played."

El Topo didn't respond. He removed a red bandanna from the back pocket of his pants and tied it around his head. The rest of the Carnales made room for him in the huddle Tulito had called together. "Do you think you can play guard? Can you dribble the ball?" Tulito asked El Topo. He answered with a smirk. "Then go in for Juan here in five minutes."

"I told him he could start in my place," Hector interrupted.

"*Nela*. We need your height up front. He'll sub for Juan."

"I ain't subbing," El Topo asserted.

"Shit, Clinto," Tulito said to Hector, throwing up his arms. "I told you this was a bad idea."

"Hey, if you guys wanna play with yourselves a little longer instead of playing some B-ball, just let me know." It was X-Lax, the designated referee, piping up.

"See that guy with the red shoes?" Hector turned El Topo around so he could look at the five Mayate players on the court. "Guard him. Get all over him, the way you were all over me that time, remember?"

El Topo shook off Hector and marched toward his assigned opponent. "Let's just give it a try," Hector pleaded with the rest of the Carnales.

Tulito shook his head and mumbled loud enough for Hector to hear, "Let's go get our *culo*s kicked."

From the sidelines, Hector watched with disbelief as, in a matter of minutes, El Topo proceeded to irritate every single player on both teams—as well as the otherwise unflappable referee. The Carnales were irritated because he took shots when he should have passed. The Mayates objected to El Topo's defensive moves, which consisted mainly of grabbing, holding, and pulling. And the referee was annoyed because both teams were suddenly asking him to monitor the game, which was something no one ever expected the person with the black whistle to do.

Hector tried to penetrate El Topo's mind, but he couldn't. The kid's brain was wired differently. On the one hand, there were some signs that El Topo was willing to join the human race. He had cooperated with the trench digging and had even showed a little competitive spirit while working. Just now he had accepted Hector's invitation to play ball. But no sooner did he take a couple of baby steps toward being a regular kid than he stepped back. There he was now, running around the court, intent on alienating himself from everyone. He was pawing, bumping, and grinning like some demented child released from an asylum. The more upset everyone got, the more El Topo seemed to enjoy himself. Why? It was as if the kid's chemistry reacted violently to even the smallest dose of kindness.

The Carnales were down two to ten when Tulito motioned for Hector to come in for Juan. Aware that the Carnales had only one sub, the Mayates were pressing full court, trying to tire everyone. Hector took the inbound pass and dribbled quickly around his defender. He waited for his teammates to find their positions. With his finger he made the signal that meant, *Let's pass the ball around until we get a good shot.* Then, out of the corner of his eye, he saw El Topo standing all alone, an easy bank shot from the net. He looked away so as to not call attention to El Topo's position while he debated whether to pass to him. In the fraction of a second before he decided, Hector thought, *If he makes a basket, maybe he'll get into the game.*

Hector's pass surprised all of the players, but most of all El Topo. The ball made a beautiful arc in the air, landed squarely on top of El Topo's flat head, and then bounced straight up. For a moment, everyone stopped and stood in silence, mesmerized by the incredible accuracy of the pass.

Then there was laughter. Loud laughter from everyone except Hector and El Topo. Hector waved at them to stop. He had a feeling that laughter would push El Topo over the edge. El Topo walked over and picked up the ball. When he turned to Hector, his grimace made Hector believe for a minute that El Topo was laughing, too. It *had* been a beautiful pass. Maybe it would be the icebreaker, the good laugh that united them as kids just playing ball, kids simply having fun. Then he saw a savage bitterness flicker on El Topo's face. El Topo raised the orange ball and, although Hector had time to raise his hands or duck, he didn't. He didn't even close his eyes, and so he saw it hurling toward him like a ball of fire. A dot as white as the midday sun filled his eyes, then it shattered into a million shards. The explosion of pain obliterated all thought. Then, gradually, he felt burning heat rush into the void in his face where his nose used to be. When he opened his eyes, Hector was surprised that he was still standing. Tulito and Juan were going after El Topo, who was being led away by couple of players from the Mayates. X-Lax was telling everyone to keep it down and chill, because if the RAs found out about any kind of clash, the basketball games would be canceled.

"Let it go," Hector managed to say to Tulito. "It's nothing."

"I hereby declare this game post-boned until tomorrow," X-Lax announced at the top of his voice.

"Hey, they should lose by default," one of the Mayate players argued. "It was their player who caused all the ruckus."

"Hey, why don't you go ruck your ass. Who's got the whistle here?" X-Lax asked with a swivel and a thrust of his hips. "The man with the whistle decides." X-Lax blew the black whistle as close to the kid's ear as he could get. "That's m-o-i, *moi*."

El Topo was deposited back in the bleachers, where he sat looking around as if he didn't know how he'd gotten there. Ronnie the RA was headed in their direction, so everyone, by silent agreement, acted as if nothing had happened. The ball started bouncing, shots were taken, rebounds were recovered.

X-Lax removed Hector's hand from his bloody face. He tweaked Hector's nose.

"Ouch," Hector groaned.

"It's not broke," X-Lax diagnosed. "It should be, but it ain't."

"It hurts like hell."

"You wanna go to the infirmary?" X-Lax asked tentatively.

The infirmary meant being treated by Colonel Taylor, which meant answering a lot of questions. "No," Hector replied.

"Let's go to the kitchen and get some ice," X-Lax recommended.

"I don't want people to see me bloody. I'll go to the room. Put on a wet rag."

"Okay. But just answer me one thing: What the hell were you trying to prove out there with El Topo?"

"I was passing him the ball."

"Not that. Why'd you ask him to play?"

"I don't know. Trying to see if the kid was mean or just stupid, I guess. Maybe this'll satisfy him." Hector patted his nose.

"No, Clinto, it won't. When a kid doesn't give a shit about pissing off the whole world, including other kids, it's a sign of worse things to come." X-Lax sighed, the weight of the past heavy in his voice. Then he turned Hector toward him. "Lemme see your pee-nocchio. The bleeding stopped. You go lie down. I'll go to the kitchen to get you some ice."

Just before he entered his dorm, Hector turned around and looked back at the basketball court. X-Lax hadn't left yet. He was still in the bleachers, having an animated, one-way conversation with El Topo. X-Lax looked like a used-car salesman making a desperate pitch. *Dumbo trying to sell something to Dumb-and-Mean,* he thought. *That should work just great.*

The following Friday morning Furman was buzzing with the news: Someone had been caught with a girl out by the back fence. Hector immediately knew it was X-Lax. He'd been planning a "date" for some time now, and he hadn't been in his bunk last night.

Yoda gave Hector all the details while he put new locks on all the doors to the dorm.

"Around midnight the alarm goes off in Colonel Taylor's quarters. He jumps out of bed and runs outside. There, by the fence, he finds them with their pants down, their asses shining in the floodlight. It was almost like they wanted to get caught."

Hector shook his head, remembering the time X-Lax had wanted him to "double-date" with him. Once again, X-Lax's brain had been short-circuited by another part of his anatomy.

"I guess they set off the alarm doing whatever it was they thought they could do through the fence," Yoda continued. "The Colonel locked them up in separate file rooms for the night."

"Them?" Hector asked. "You mean the girl, too?"

"No, the girls must have run off. I mean X-Lax and El

Topo. This morning the Colonel drove them to the Okee-chobee Juvenile Detention Center. I feel sorry for them—I've heard that isn't a pretty place."

"What?" Hector was incredulous. "X-Lax and *El Topo?* Are you sure?"

"Yeah, I was surprised, too," Yoda said. "I can understand X-Lax sneaking out by himself, horny toad that he is, but I didn't think he was friends with El Topo."

"He wasn't," said Hector.

The next day Hector got a letter. He read it alone in his room.

Hey, Clinto:

This is my last night at Furman. Chicken Wings is sending me off to Okeechobee in the morning, so I'm slipping this note in with the mail. Don't worry about me. I can do three months there easy. It was worth it, Clinto. Even a tiny taste of Bobbie's sweet lovin' is worth three months there and more. And you, amigo, *owe me* MUCHO *for gettin' El Topo out of your short hairs. I'll send you the bill sometime. P.S. You can keep my fan. Sansón gets my boom box, and the magazines and pictures go to Yoda. Tell him not to sue me if they give him a heart attack.*

X-Lax

Angry as he was at X-Lax's incredibly dumb move, Hector couldn't help but laugh. X-Lax had sacrificed himself for Hector, but at least he'd gone down with a smile.

8

Two months later, Hector, Sansón, Tulito, and Juan are in Hector's room. Tulito and Juan are sitting on the bottom bunk, which has been empty since X-Lax was sent away. Hector and Sansón are on the desk chairs. Having just finished reading a children's version of *Don Quijote,* Sansón and Tulito are engaging in one of their inevitable literary discussions.

"It's sad to see Don Quijote come back home and die, realizing he's not a knight, just a crazy old man," Tulito claims.

Sansón, on the other hand, thinks Cervantes meant the ending to be happy. "*La verdad* is always good, *ése*."

"But just because something's good doesn't mean it's happy," argues Tulito.

Sansón can't find the words to counter Tulito.

Hector himself doesn't know whether the book's ending is happy or sad. It's sad that Don Quijote loses the illusion of being a knight, but it's good that he discovers who he is, even if he's just an ordinary man. Hector resolves to check out the adult, unabridged version of the book to see how that ending reads. This is what he's thinking when Ronnie the RA pops his head in and tells Hector that the Colonel wants to see him.

Sitting in a chair in front of Taylor's desk is a man who from the back looks like Hector's high school teacher Mr. Ortíz. He stands up and turns around when he hears Hector come in.

"Manuel Martínez," says the man, stretching out his hand. His strong grip holds Hector until Hector gives him his name.

"Hector," Colonel Taylor says when they all take seats, "Mr. Martínez is here from SMU, Southern Methodist University, outside of Dallas. You may have heard of it."

Hector nods, but in fact he hasn't.

"He's here to offer you the chance to enroll."

It's Colonel Taylor's style to cut to the chase, as he likes to say. Hector just sits there, stunned.

Mr. Martínez shifts in his chair to speak to Hector. "The Colonel here wrote me a letter about you. He and I know each other from the air force. He was my captain."

"I was your colonel . . . and still am."

Martínez grins. "Excuse me, sir. I meant that you were my captain when I first joined your squadron. When we parted company, he was my colonel and I was his sergeant. He's everyone's colonel now, as you know."

Hector knows.

"Anyway, like I said, Colonel Taylor wrote me about you. He sent me your transcript and your SAT scores. You're an exceptional student."

"He's the best we've had," says Colonel Taylor matter-of-factly. This is news to Hector.

"I'll come to the point, just like the Colonel did. You're the kind of student we'd like to have at SMU. We want to offer you a scholarship. Full tuition and living expenses for four years."

Hector remains silent. He took the SATs at Mrs. Pana's insistence, but he never filled out the college applications she had given him.

"What are your plans? What do you want to do?" Mr. Martínez probes.

Plans. The word sounds almost foreign. When he arrived at Furman, the thought of planning anything had seemed pointless. Making plans requires having hope. Over time Hector had slowly, cautiously begun to think about the future without fear of hurt and disappointment.

But Mr. Martínez used a word that feels even stranger than *plans.* The word that scares him is *want.* For a long time all he wanted was to be left in peace, to live each day without dread. With El Topo out of his life, Hector can breathe again. How could he allow himself to want anything more? Now there is room in his head for thoughts about people back home, like Aurora, Conchita—even Sandra—and sometimes he dares to dream a little about the future. But how do you know that what you want is what you *really* want, or that what you want is the *right thing* to want? *Want* is a word he struggles and wrestles with constantly.

"What do I want?" he asks out loud, more to himself than to anyone else.

"What do you want to do?"

Hector is silent again. There is no need to hurry. The Colonel and Mr. Martínez will wait for his answer. He shuts his eyes, takes a deep breath, and feels the air travel through his nostrils, down his esophagus, and into his abdomen. He lets it out slowly, counting the beats like Díaz taught him. He turns on his mental flashlight and it illuminates many scenes:

> *The girl with the goofy glasses, who gave the unforgettable*
> *speech at the Lions Club.*
>
> *Conchita on her bed, surrounded by letters.*
>
> *Aurora on the basketball court, telling him not to give up.*
>
> *Sansón reading third-grade books all on his own.*
>
> *Papá digging in his garden.*
>
> *Filiberto handing him the savings-account book.*
>
> *X-Lax gesticulating to El Topo in the bleachers.*
>
> *Díaz in his cell, saying, "I like it here."*

These memories guide his words and actions. Now he is ready to speak.

"To be honest with you," he says to Mr. Martínez, "I don't know that much about SMU. I need more time to figure out what I want to do . . . for a living, with my life. I'd like some time to think about what I would study if I went to college."

The surprise is evident on Mr. Martínez's face. "But you've put in your time here. You can move on now."

Hector nods, but he doesn't say any more.

"If you take too long to decide, you'll miss the enrollment deadline. Then what will you do? Where will you go?"

Hector wonders in a detached way why Mr. Martínez is so eager, so anxious. Does he have a quota to fill?

Colonel Taylor leans forward in his chair. "Martínez, why don't you give him one of those brochures with the pretty coeds on the cover. He can look through it, do some more thinking. We'll get in touch with you as soon as we're ready."

Hector smiles a little at Colonel Taylor's use of the word *we*.

Manuel Martínez takes out a folder with Hector's name on it. "Here's my number," he says, pointing to the business card stapled to a corner of the folder. "Don't let this slip through your fingers. This is an incredible opportunity, one that doesn't come along every day."

After Mr. Martínez leaves, Colonel Taylor closes his office door. He grabs Hector by the shoulders and turns him around to face him. "You take your time, you hear?"

"Actually," says Hector, "I don't need any more time. I know what I want to do—next year, at least."

9

Hector's playing chess with Dr. Luna the Lunatic. He thinks, *If I don't focus, Luna will win for the first time.* On various occasions he has been on the verge of letting Luna win, just so the guy won't get discouraged. But in every instance he has been unable to do it. Dr. Luna's just too much of a dork.

One of the reasons Hector is distracted is that as soon as he finishes with Dr. Luna, he's off to outside detail. He'll drive a John Deere 5510 with a mower attached and get paid for doing it. The thing is sleek. The best part is that the tractor has been retrofitted with two balancers so it can mow vertical slopes without tipping over.

Hector is considered a good worker because he takes an outside job every chance he gets. People are amazed that the sun and the heat don't bother him. He puts on his blue cap with the white *F*—which stands for Furman, not what X-Lax said—and off he goes. Hector doesn't think of himself as a great worker. He just likes driving the tractor sideways and whacking weeds with the gas-powered Super Whacker. It is good work for thinking.

"May I ask," says Dr. Luna out of the blue, "why you decided to stay at Furman?"

"Sure." Hector reminds himself to be careful. Luna sometimes starts a conversation just to get his mind off the game. Whenever Luna asks a question about his life, Hector automatically scans the board for the piece that Luna's lusting after.

"So, why?"

"I figure this place needs all the help it can get." Hector moves his queen one square.

Luna chuckles. "You got that right. And SMU?"

"It'll still be there next year."

"You know," Dr. Luna says, knotting his hands behind his head in surrender, "you don't have to come see me anymore. You graduated. You're an RA now. You're free."

Free. Hector savors the word for a moment. In an instant he imagines his father on the white *yegüita*, galloping *como el propio viento.* They are moving so fast that his father and the white horse seem one. *Como un centauro,* he thinks.

Then he says, "I'll stop coming when you beat me."

The last time they met, Dr. Luna had asked Hector in the middle of the game to close his eyes and tell him what he saw right then and there. When Hector obliged, he saw Taco leaping and bounding out of nowhere, his tail whipping around, just like when his father whistled for him. Only this time it was Mamá calling him. It was early in the morning, just before Mass. Mamá was feeding him leftovers out by the back door. All along she complained about Taco, that he was a pain, doing his business where people stepped, getting ticks and fleas on people's hair, and there she was, feeding him with her own two hands.

"Was this before or after your father died?" Dr. Luna had asked gently.

"I can't remember," said Hector.

"Try to go back there again," said Luna.

This time Hector saw him, his father. He was in the kitchen, out of sight, quietly observing Conchita. He looked happy. Truly happy and at peace.

So, of course, Lunatic had wanted to know the significance of the memory. But just then Hector saw Luna's bishop waiting to pounce on his king, so all he said was

"I'm glad I remembered it." He didn't want Dr. Luna to win or to get too carried away with the psychologizing.

After he beats Luna yet again, Hector waits outside for the van to pick him up. From his pocket he pulls a tattered paperback and cracks it open. Inside is X-Lax's latest letter, which he's using as a bookmark. X-Lax has written Hector two other times. He got out of Okeechobee intact, although there were some close calls. He and El Topo had been separated when they got to Okeechobee. Apparently El Topo was assigned to the boot-camp unit, the absolute last hope for the hopeless. X-Lax wrote, *They'll either kill him or turn him into a future Norton.*

X-Lax is now working in a small amusement park outside of Houston, as the attendant in charge of the bumper cars. He's living with Bobbie and her friend Yvette, all three of them in a trailer not much bigger than Díaz's cell. It sounds to Hector as though X-Lax has finally landed in his idea of heaven.

Sansón had also decided to stay on at Furman for another year, as Yoda's assistant. He and Hector are co-teaching the dumbbells course. Ten kids signed up at the beginning, and they figure they'll end up with two. The program with Díaz was canceled right after their visit to the prison. According to the Colonel, a state senator complained about the money being spent to bring convicts to Furman, and that was the end of that. As soon as Hector gets his driver's license, the Colonel will lend him the Dodge Ram so he and Sansón can drive over to the penitentiary.

Through the fence at the end of the parking lot, Hector sees one of his students dragging a bulky garbage bag to the cafeteria's dumpster. Heaven forbid that he should lift it. The kid is a rough-looking, tattooed kid from Houston who calls himself Pelón. He reminds Hector of El Topo. Pelón's first night at Furman, Hector gave him a demerit for fighting with his roommate. It's been a month now, and Pelón is still cursing under his breath, but he hasn't earned any more demerits. Maybe he'll make it. You can't make it at Furman unless you put some effort into it, even if it's just the effort to fake it. So, either he hates wherever he came from so much that he doesn't want to be sent back, or, maybe, just maybe, somewhere deep inside his sorry ass there is a drop of good. Hector looks forward to finding out.

The van enters the parking lot. Hector slips the book back in his pocket. He'll read it during his break. Or maybe he'll use the time to write to Aurora. He'd like to send her some money so she could come for a visit. Not Mamá—not yet—just Aurora.

For now, his tractor awaits.